the
ghosts
of
normal

Also by Allison Burnett

Christopher
The House Beautiful
Death By Sunshine
The Escape of Malcolm Poe
Undiscovered Gyrl
Another Girl

the ghosts of normal

Allison Burnett

Copyright © 2020 by Allison Burnett

All Rights Reserved. No part of this book may be reproduced without written permission from the writer.

This is a work of fiction. Names, characters, places, and incidents are either the products of the author's imagination or used fictitiously. Any resemblance to actual persons, living or dead, or actual events is entirely coincidental.

ISBN: 9798699066124

Cover design by Jeremy Milks
Cover photography by David King Lassman
Book design by Amy Inouye

Printed in the United States of America

For my boys, Keats and Winslow

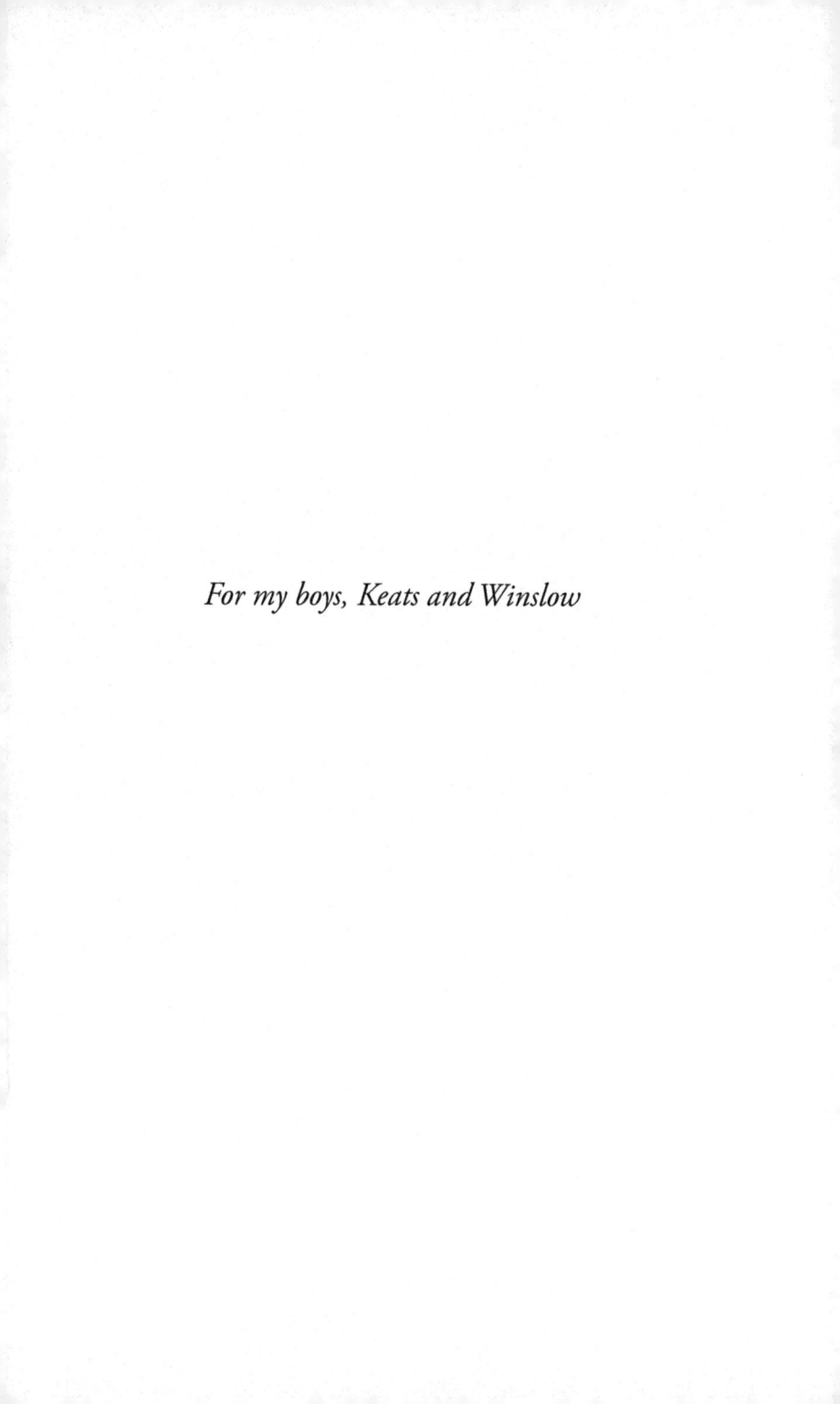

*He was part of my dream, of course—
but then I was part of his dream, too!*

—Lewis Carroll

1.

SINCE MOVING TO TOWN at the start of the school year, Max Beatty had yet to make a single friend. Even now, as he walked home at the end of a long school day, his classmates streamed past him without so much as a glance in his direction, as though he were invisible. And no wonder. Ever since his father had died the year before, Max had pretty much stopped talking. In the beginning, kids teased him about his shyness, asking if he spoke English or even had vocal cords, but soon they grew bored and moved on to other targets. Now he was worse than disliked. He was nothing.

Approaching a red-brick church, Max saw a dented beer can lying on a low pile of dead, wet leaves. Without thinking, he kicked the can as hard as he could, and then, after he had caught up with it, kicked it again. He would try to kick it all the way to his front door. A stupid game, but it was better than feeling lonely.

Suddenly, a harsh voice tore the air: "The new graphics are lit! People explode right in front of you. Blood and guts everywhere. I can't believe it's even legal."

Max whipped around. Two boys were cutting across the street ahead of him. The loud one was Tim Schmidt, a stocky kid with a crew-cut and ears that stuck out, who had been held back a year and liked to shout disgusting compliments at girls. Max had heard his mother was in jail for robbing a gas station and wouldn't get out until Tim was twenty. Tim's friend was Eddie Wong, who was big and strong and knew martial arts. Even though he could break you in half with his bare hands, he was actually pretty nice when Tim wasn't around.

Max waited for them to pass. His heart beat quickly. He didn't want them to see his can.

After they had turned down an alleyway, he pulled back his foot to kick again.

A shout rang out: "Hey, Beatty!"

Max froze, startled.

Magically, Tim and Eddie were standing right in front of him, smiling as though he were their best friend.

"Wanna come over and play video games?" Tim asked.

"Please?" Eddie said, putting his big hands together in prayer.

Max blinked, his face turning red. No one had ever asked him to do anything after school. His eyes brightened, but before he could speak, the truth slapped him hard across the face. The boys were gone. They had cut down the alleyway and never come back.

He had just imagined them.

Since the death of his father, Max's brain had been playing tricks. At first, he had thought it was just some sort of glitch that would fix itself, but now, months later, it was only getting worse. In the beginning he could tell what was real and what wasn't; now, more and more often, he was fooled. Was this how a person went crazy? he wondered. Slowly at first, then one day you woke up in a mental hospital? Angry that he even had to ask the question, he kicked the can as hard as he could and walked away, toward the public library.

In Waterville, the town where Max was born, the library was a proud brick building with white marble steps, giant iron lamps, and 1899 chiseled above the door. Its ceilings were so high that it was like stepping into a church. Here, the library was the complete opposite—low, flat, modern, and boring. The floors were covered with grey carpet, and the walls and windows were so thin they shook whenever a truck drove past. But Max didn't care. All that mattered were the books, and there were enough here to keep him busy for a hundred years.

After a ten-minute search, Max spotted what he was looking for. He went up on tiptoe and stretched as far as he could. His fingers tickled the book's spine, but he couldn't grab hold of it. Just as he was about to give up and find a stool, a long, veiny hand appeared out of nowhere, grasped the book, and brought it down.

"Awful big book for a little fella," said a deep voice.

Max looked up into one of the oldest faces he had ever seen. But it wasn't ugly. Amidst all the wrinkles shone a warm smile and gentle blue eyes. Thinking fast, Max glanced away, then back again. The old man was still there. He was definitely real. Before Max could gather the courage to thank him for his help, the old man dropped his hand to his wooden cane and spoke.

"When I was your age," he said, "I loved history, too. I had no choice. I was born into it. On Black Tuesday, to be precise. October 29, 1929. The day the stock market crashed. The beginning of The Great Depression. Everybody was poor. All we had was each other. Then, when I wasn't much older than you are, the Japanese attacked Pearl Harbor. Overnight, a world war began. A terrible time. I grew up with the sort of fear you never forget."

His eyes caught the sunlight, and suddenly Max could picture what he looked like when he was a boy. He thought he could even see the fear. Max took a deep breath, determined to tell the old man that he knew a lot about World War Two, had read a book about D-Day, and had seen a long black-and-white movie with his dad once, about what it was like to come home after the war ended. Before Max could spit it out, the old man, unaware of Max's difficulty with speech, patted him on the head and walked away.

"You wasted too much time deciding what to eat," Eddie Wong said, munching corn chips. "Now we got less than an hour to play. My mom said if I'm even a minute late, I lose my phone for a week."

Tim Schmidt took a swig of his energy drink, then wiped his red mouth with his sleeve. "What a bunch of crap. She's bluffing and you know it."

"I dunno, man. She went berserk over my C on the book report."

A car horn blared.

Tim turned around and shouted, *"Look!"*

He pointed to the middle of the street, where a little brown dog was trapped in traffic. Cars and trucks, sweeping around a bend, didn't have time to brake, so they were forced to swerve. The animal spun in a tight, frantic circle, afraid to take a step.

"I'm a dog person," Tim said with a devilish smile, as he dug into his bag of spicy chips. "I bet you didn't know that." He ran to the curb and dangled one as bait. "Here, boy! Come on, boy! It's delicious!"

"What're you doing?" Eddie asked.

"Come get it!

Hearing the friendly voice, the dog was tempted to make a run for it.

"Stop it!" Eddie cried. "You'll get him run over!"

Eddie tried to grab the chip, but Tim laughed and snatched it away.

A loud screech.

The boys turned their heads.

A car had skidded to a stop. The driver blasted his horn.

Tim jumped off the curb, waving the chip again. "That's right, come on, boy! *Come on!*"

Trusting the voice, the animal made a mad dash for it. At the same time, a car sped up from the other direction. The driver, surprised, slammed on his brakes, but too late. As the dog flew through the air, its yelp sounded almost human. It landed with a hard smack against the curb. Almost immediately, it regained its feet, but its rear right leg dangled, hopelessly broken. It whimpered as it limped away.

"Look what you did!" Eddie screamed.

"I didn't do anything," Tim said, his voice shaky. "The car did it."

He grabbed his friend by the arm and pulled him in the opposite direction.

"Shouldn't we call the police or something?" Eddie said.

"What for? It's just a stray. Don't be such a god-damn snowflake."

Max was sitting on a bench, inspecting photographs of Civil War generals when he heard the whimper. He looked up and spotted the dog, hobbling into the shadows that filled the park at sunset. Max jumped up and opened his mouth to cry for help, but no sound came. He dropped his book on the bench and ran as fast as he could. It took him less than a minute to corner the dog against a wall of shrubbery. Seeing how scared it was, Max fell to his knees.

"I won't hurt you," he whispered. "I promise. I just want to help."

Max reached out a hand. When his fingers were just inches from its collar, the dog darted into the bushes. Max dove in after him. He followed its tail as the animal pushed through the hedge. Max crawled over stones and trash, through sharp branches, until he reached an old picket fence. He shoved aside some rotten boards and broke through to the other side. When he stood up, his hands and face were filthy and scratched.

Above him loomed a tall, wooden house. The sinking sun threw blinding light across its high gables. A long time ago, it must have caught fire, because the roof was charred black and the windows were clouded with soot. Max spotted the dog sitting on the back porch beneath a "No Trespassing" sign. The sign had been ignored at least once, because the back door was half open. As Max approached the dog, a chilly wind blew leaves across the yard. A shutter slammed overhead. Max wanted to run away, but he knew if he left the dog alone and it died, he would never forgive himself.

He knelt down and extended a hand.

"Don't be scared," he said.

The frightened animal shrank away, dragging its broken leg. It was clearly in pain, trembling violently. Max mounted the first step. A creak. He heard a low moan overhead. He looked up at the house, half-expecting to have called forth demons, but nothing had changed. It was just the wind in the trees. He climbed the second step. Another creak. The wood was so old and weak, he worried it might break. He reached out both hands for the animal.

The dog met his eyes, then bolted for the back door. Max lunged and his shoe slipped. He fell face down. The instant his elbows landed, lights popped on in the downstairs windows and a trumpet blared inside. Terrified, Max threw himself off the porch and ran as fast as his legs could carry him.

2.

A GIANT MAN who overheated quickly, Jim Jarvis had ripped off his clip-on tie and popped open a beer the minute he got home from work. Bluish smoke rose from his cigarette and coiled around his head like a serpent as he watched the evening news. He was in a foul mood. It had been another lousy day of driving in circles for hours, in search of a house he could buy cheap, fix up fast, and sell for a profit. With prices going up all the time, there wasn't a single property he could afford. And now even the simple pleasure of a nice, cold beer was being ruined by the thump of a bass drum from downstairs. He mashed out his cigarette and strode in heavy boots to the basement door.

"That's it!" he shouted. "Party's over! Send 'em home!"

The music abruptly stopped.

Jim's new wife, Caroline, emerged from the kitchen, holding a long wooden spoon. Her hair was dirty blonde and as thin as corn silk.

"What's the matter, babe?" she asked.

"God damn music! At least at my place, he was out

in the garage. Here, it's like it's playing in my skull."

Caroline screwed up her delicate, heart-shaped face as she considered the problem of Jim's son and his rock band. "Maybe we can soundproof the ceiling or something."

"You wanna pay for that? I don't. I've got a better idea. Let 'im move out and find a place of his own. He's twenty-three, for Christ's sake. When I was his age, I was driving a forklift. I had a place of my own."

Behind them, the front door burst open, and Max entered, breathing hard, red-cheeked, his pale face trickling blood. His thick, brown hair was matted. He thumped his backpack to the floor and stared at his mother, his eyes as wide as could be.

"Sweetie, what's the matter?" Caroline said. "What happened? You're all scratched up!"

He wanted to tell her all about the injured dog and the haunted house, but his stepfather was right there, smirking at him. Jim's face, even when it was smiling, was more terrifying to Max than a knife or a loaded gun.

Caroline laid a hand on his forehead, pushing back his damp hair. "Oh, baby, you're burning up."

"Guess we'd better call the fire department," Jim said.

Max tried to look at him but couldn't. Whenever their eyes met, Max felt like his body was shriveling up, and he could hardly breathe.

Caroline turned Max's shoulders toward the stairs. "Straight into the tub, young man."

Without a word, Max bounded up the stairs, two at a time.

Jim shook his head. "I swear, he gets freakier by the minute."

Caroline winced. "Please don't say that."

Jim snorted a laugh and walked back to the television.

Even though it had been four months since they'd moved to town, Max still didn't feel at home there. It wasn't the new house, which was actually much bigger and better than the old place. It was the people who lived inside it. For Max's whole life, the Beattys had been a family of four; Max, his dad, his mom, and his sister Sally. Then his father had drowned in Eagle Lake, and, not even six months later, his mother had announced that she was getting married again. It was a terrible shock, made even more terrible by her choice of husband. Jim Jarvis had been his dad's business partner. She had never even told Max they were dating.

The night his mother and Jim made the announcement, instead of eating the celebratory cake she served, Max ran to his room and cried for hours. His sister Sally couldn't understand why. Sure, Jim was disgusting, arrogant, and stupid, but was it really worth having a breakdown over? Mom was an adult and had the right to marry whoever she wanted, didn't she? Max knew Sally was right, but it didn't lessen the pain.

In the months leading up to the wedding, Max begged his mother to cancel it, but whenever she asked him why, he couldn't offer her a reason. He simply fell silent. In the end, Caroline decided his rejection of Jim was nothing more than a boy's blind loyalty to his father, and she went ahead with their plans.

That July, two weeks after a humble backyard ceremony, the family moved an hour away. Max wasn't surprised that Jim had invited his son Paul to move in with them. Even though he was, indeed, too old to be sleeping in anyone's basement, he had been sleeping in Jim's his entire life. As he was broke, and his rock band, "Colony Collapse Disorder," had yet to land a paying gig, his dependency might as well continue. But then a week later, the band's lead singer, Paul's girlfriend Angela, lost her job at the pancake house, and she too moved in. Overnight it seemed, a family of three had doubled to six, and almost no one got along. Was it any wonder Max spent as much time out of the new house as possible?

That night when Max sat down at the dinner table, his hair still wet from the bath, his mother was in the middle of singing her stepson's praises: "Oh, Angie, it's a shame you slept in. You should have seen Paul, all cleaned up for work with his dad. His beard trimmed. His hair brushed. He looked so handsome."

"Made him take out his earrings, too," Jim said.

"Why?" Angela asked, genuinely curious.

"Once he's paying his own way, I don't care if he wears a dress and high heels. But if he's gonna work with me and live under my roof—"

"You mean my mom's roof," Sally corrected, not even looking up from her novel.

Ever since she was a little girl, Sally had been allowed to read during family meals. Even though it was bad manners, Caroline made an exception because Sally was a straight-A student, headed for college one day.

Feeling Jim's anger, Sally lifted her calm, grey eyes and met his glare.

"What?" she said. "It's the truth. She pays the rent, not you. You pay for zero."

"Sweetheart, please," Caroline pleaded. "We're married now. What's mine is Jim's, and what's Jim's is mine."

"While that's legally true, it's ridiculous. You have Dad's insurance money and the money from selling our house. What does he have except a garbage attitude and a broken-down van?"

Caroline peeked over at her husband, afraid he might erupt, but instead he was grinning at Sally.

"Stupid kid. What do you know about true love?" He leaned over, yanked his bride close, and buried his scratchy cheek into her neck, making her giggle.

Max watched him closely. When his father had kissed his mother, it wasn't rough like this. It was sweet and gentle and made everyone happy. Max's eyes drifted away, and his mind returned to the worries that had burdened him since getting home. Had lights really turned on in the windows of the old house or had he just imagined them? And what about the blast of the trumpet? Had he imagined that too? Both had seemed real. As real as his own heartbeat.

Whenever Max couldn't sleep, he took out the fancy pencils and notepad his mom had bought him last Christmas and sketched until he got drowsy. That night, sitting up in bed, his heart anxiously fluttering, Max sketched a portrait of the little dog. Its beard was difficult—all those coarse brown hairs poking out in a thousand different directions—but he had gotten the eyes just right. Damp and brown, they seemed to reach off the page, begging for help.

The door opened. "Hey, Maxie."

Angela was the only person who'd ever called him that, and for some reason he really loved it. He also loved her perfect white smile, her wavy hair that smelled like flowers, and how she never seemed worried about anything.

"I have an awesome idea," she said, sitting down next to him. "What if someday soon we drive up to Harms Woods to see the leaves? Would you like that? I hear they're screaming their heads off these days."

Max screwed up his face as though she were insane. "Leaves can't scream."

These were the first words he had spoken to a human

being all day, and his voice sounded hoarse and strange even to himself.

"They're screaming with *color*. They're saying, 'Look at me! No, no! Look at me! *Me!* Over here!'"

Max laughed—a sweet, little trill.

Paul appeared at the door, wearing a brown leather jacket, creased everywhere, with fur at the collar.

"Ready?" he asked.

"We're going to a movie," Angela explained as she kissed Max's cheek. "Sweet dreams."

Max swiftly tore a page from his pad and handed it to her.

"For me?"

He nodded.

She smiled into the dog's eyes. "It's beautiful. Thank you."

She walked away, stroking a hand across Paul's stomach as she passed.

Paul lingered, his hand on the doorknob. "How you doin', squirt?"

Max just stared at him.

"Yeah," Paul sighed, "that's what I figured."

Downstairs, buttoning her coat, Angela heard muffled voices in the dining room. She peered around the corner and saw Jim sitting in his undershirt, drinking a beer with a red-haired man who was almost as tall as he was, but even bigger. His fat, freckled arms were covered with tattoos.

"You sure he wants to sell?" Jim muttered.

"I heard him tell his lawyer. He hasn't even hired a real estate agent yet, but, yeah, that's the plan."

A smile spread across Jim's face like a stain. He lifted his beer bottle and clinked it against his friend's.

Paul was suddenly at Angela's ear. "We're gonna be late."

In the car, Angela realized that she was still holding the drawing Max had given her. She studied it more closely, losing herself.

"He's so talented," she said finally. "Most kids his age draw stick figures."

"You've known him a few months, and you get presents," Paul said. "I practically watched him grow up, and I get nothing."

"You're impatient with him."

"Oh, come on. He's barely said a word since his father died. Is that my fault?"

Angela repeated the word with even more weight: *"Impatient."*

3.

MISS ROLAND, a stern African-American educator who wore colorful scarves around her head and noisy gold bangles on her wrists, addressed a class of fourth-graders. While most of the students paid only scant or restless attention to what she was saying, Max was deeply, genuinely interested in every word. Not only was Miss Roland his favorite teacher, but Social Studies his favorite subject.

"You've all read Chapter Nine," she said. "How about regurgitating some of it for me? What'd you learn about Andrew Jackson? Anyone?"

Silence.

She made her eyes go dead. "Oh, so it's going to be like that?" She pointed a pretty, red fingernail at a grumpy girl with bangs so long it was a wonder she could even see. "Miss Dupree, give me a fact, any fact."

"Andrew Jackson was the seventh president of the United States."

"Okay. What else? Mr. Petrowski?"

Griffin Petrowski, a gangly boy with pointy ears and a sneaky smile, raised his hand and shouted, "He had white hair!"

Everybody laughed. It didn't matter that what he had said was not at all funny. The class clown must be encouraged.

Miss Roland scanned worried faces. "Anyone else?"

Tim Schmidt shouted out: "He's on the twenty-dollar bill. I'm gonna have a million of 'em someday."

"You plan to rob a bank?"

Max, sitting in the last row, couldn't help but smile. Unlike most teachers, Miss Roland didn't pretend to like every student. Tim was a jerk, and that was how she treated him.

Miss Roland saw Max's appreciation of her remark. "Anything to add, Mr. Beatty?"

Max was startled. Knowing how shy he was, she almost never called on him. Thanks to his new library book, Max knew far more about Andrew Jackson than what was written in Chapter Nine of their textbook. He took a deep breath and tried to speak. His face grew red. He gripped the sides of his desk. Nothing came.

Tim Schmidt wheeled around and announced, "Ladies and gentlemen, the Amazing Blabbermouth!"

The room exploded with laughter.

Tim leaned over and slapped hands with Eddie Wong.

Max dropped his head as the laughter washed over him in waves. He endured the humiliation for what seemed like forever, until, unable to bear it a moment longer, he popped to his feet, his voice loud and strong: "Before he was president . . . when he was just a general . . . Andrew Jackson and his men killed 186 Creek Indians at Tallushatchee. Davy Crockett bragged, 'We shot 'em like dogs!'"

The class was stunned into silence, and so Max continued:

"Later, Andrew Jackson won the Red Stick War at Horseshoe Bend. The peace treaty afterwards stole twenty million acres of land from the Creek Indians. Once he was president, he was even worse to the Native Americans. He . . . he—"

Max stopped to catch his breath. His classmates were turned around in their chairs, staring at him, wide eyed. Max was smarter than they knew. He was probably the smartest kid in the school.

An instant later, like a bubble bursting, the faces of the children vanished. Again, Max saw just the backs of their heads, shaking as they laughed at Tim's stupid joke.

Max had not uttered a word.

"Suit yourself," Miss Roland sighed, with a touch of disappointment. "Miss Tabor? Tell me something about our eighth president, Martin Van Buren."

By the ring of the final bell, word had spread around the school that Max had almost fainted in class, trying to speak. Trudging home in misery, his backpack as heavy as an anchor, Max was startled by the sound of Tim Schmidt's voice:

"Hey, Beatty, I got a question for you! Are you deaf and dumb, or just crazy like your old man?"

Tim was standing at the corner with Eddie Wong.

"His dad's crazy?" Eddie asked Tim, genuinely surprised.

"*Was.* He's dead now. My mom says he *musta* been nuts to do what he did."

"What'd he do?"

"Drowned himself. Jumped in Eagle Lake."

Outraged, Max ran up, eyes flashing, and lunged at Tim with both hands.

Tim stepped aside like a matador and watched Max flop to the grass.

"You think you can kick my ass?" Tim said. "You're *definitely* insane."

The boys laughed and walked away.

Struggling to his feet, his backpack turned around, Max knew there was only one way to redeem this miserable day.

Fighting tears, he took off running toward the park.

When he arrived at the wall of shrubbery, he was shocked to see that it was perfectly intact, as though he had never tunneled through it. Remembering how badly he had been scratched, Max ran to the back of the park and down an alleyway until he reached a rickety, old gate.

He ventured inside.

The house was just as he had left it the day before,

except, with the sun higher in the sky, it seemed far less scary. More than anything else, it looked sad, like a grave no one ever visited. Hoping that he had merely imagined the lights and the trumpet, he walked over, held his breath, and laid his sneaker on the bottom step.

No creak this time.

He took the next step.

Nothing.

He laid his foot on the porch. The lights flashed exactly as before, but this time instead of a single trumpet, a few instruments blasted.

Max screamed, jumped off the steps, and ran.

Halfway across the yard, he stopped dead in his tracks. He thought of the little dog—its dangling leg, its frightened eyes, and how it had trembled from head to toe. He couldn't give up now. He had to save its life.

Max turned around slowly, bravely, like a man of honor who, having counted out the steps of a duel, was ready to kill or be killed. What was he afraid of, anyway? Lights and music never hurt anyone. He ran back and mounted the first step.

Nothing.

Second step.

Nothing.

The porch.

Lights, music!

He lifted his foot. The windows went black and the music stopped. The only sound was a far-away siren. He stepped on and off the porch three times. Each time, the lights and music popped on and off. If anyone lived in the house, they probably thought he was the most annoying person in the world.

He decided that before he barged in through the open back door, he would knock on the front door and see what happened. He found a cement pathway, overgrown with weeds, and followed it. He stopped when the weeds grew so tall that he would have needed a machete to hack through. He was about to turn around when he heard two familiar voices coming from out front. Scarcely able to believe what his ears were telling him, he dropped to all fours and crawled through the overgrowth. It was scratchy, painful, and smelly, but he had to know. At the end, he parted the weeds like curtains. There, twenty feet away, standing on the lifeless lawn, were two filthy, brown boots. Looming above them, blocking out the sun, was his stepfather.

"What's the difference between a rich man and a poor man?" Jim asked.

Max heard Paul answer glumly, "Money."

"Nope. *Vision*. I've got vision. Do you? Tell me what you see."

"A burned-out ruin."

"I see a gold mine."

"You're kidding, right?"

"All that black? That's just smoke damage. Superficial. The walls are sound. That's why it was never condemned.

I'll remodel—carve it up into six units, two per floor. I'll triple my money."

"It's not even for sale."

"Wanna bet?"

"There's no sign."

"I got an inside tip. Some old guy owns it. He's like a hundred. It's been empty forever. But he's ready to sell. To the right buyer. He wants a family man."

"That's you?"

"Uh-huh."

"Excuse me while I barf."

"You'll see, smart ass."

After Max heard Jim's truck drive away, he turned and crawled back the way he'd come. So no one lived in the house. That meant he had nothing to be afraid of but his own imagination. He ran over and jumped onto the back porch. The lights and music popped on. Pretending it hadn't happened, he strode to the door, opened it wide, and entered.

What Max saw took his breath away. Golden sunlight poured through the clear windows of an old-fashioned kitchen. The antique refrigerator, stove, and sink were sparkling white. The floor was laid with tiny, geometric marble tiles. A pie lay cooling on the windowsill. No trace of fire anywhere, not even the smell. He was startled by what sounded like a tiny rooster crow. A door swung open and the little dog pushed its way in, tail wagging.

Before Max could even react, it scampered over and threw its paws up onto his knees. Its hind leg wasn't broken anymore. How could that be? Max looked at the ceiling and quickly down again. It wasn't his imagination. The dog was real, and its leg was completely healed. As though the creature sensed his astonishment, it scampered back to the swinging door and bounced in place, urging Max to see for himself the answers that lay beyond.

4.

WHEN MAX PUSHED OPEN the swinging door, he expected to see evidence of the fire. It was astonishing enough that the kitchen had been untouched by the flames, but, given the state of the house's exterior, for the rest of the house to have also been spared was simply unimaginable. Yet that's what he discovered. It was nothing short of a miracle: there was no sign of a fire; not even of passing time. It was like a perfect museum of the past, or like a day from long ago trapped inside a dream. Everything was old but at the same time beautiful and new. The music he had heard outside was audible but softer, coming from somewhere deep in the house.

Impatient, the dog darted between Max's legs and trotted down a long, flowery carpet all the way to the front door, where it turned around and sat, tail thumping, waiting for him to follow.

Max entered. After just a few steps, the music abruptly stopped. Max froze, listening intently. No voices. No one approached. Only the tiny tick-tock of a clock and, somewhere, the brush of a branch against a windowpane.

He started to walk again. The crystals of a table lamp threw the colors of the rainbow along a wall. On a little desk stood a stand-up telephone with an earpiece—the kind he had seen in old movies. He reached a towering grandfather clock with a smiling-moon face and a brass eagle on its head. The pendulum swayed with steady calm. Who had wound it? To his right stood a dining room table, set with white lace and silver candlesticks. In the distance, the music started up again, even happier and livelier than before. The dog squirmed, beating its tail faster on the floor. Finally, unable to contain its enthusiasm, it darted through an archway into the living room. Max drew a deep breath and followed.

Arranged around a tiled fireplace were two overstuffed sofas, a rocking chair, a crammed bookcase, and a wooden radio with legs. A folded newspaper lay on a small table. Max opened it. November 11, 1938. Strangely, it looked perfect, as though it had just been delivered and not yet read. An ugly squawk made him jump. The music was coming from behind a pair of French doors, slightly ajar, at the end of the room. As Max warily approached them, he realized the music wasn't recorded; there were too many weird, funny notes for it to be professional. It was being played live, and at least one of the musicians was terrible.

He peeked between the doors.

A few yards away, a stocky, bald man with rolled-up sleeves played the trumpet, his face red, his cheeks puffed out, his round glasses slightly foggy. Behind him, a woman with bushy blonde hair played an upright piano, her hands quick and expert. Max craned his neck and saw a skinny, old man, wearing a vest and a bowtie, plucking the thick strings of a stand-up bass. A hideous shriek pulled Max's eyes to a boy about his own age seated on a hard-backed chair, making pained faces as he blew into a clarinet.

There was no way these people were real, Max decided. Either he was asleep and dreaming, or he was awake and totally insane. A third possibility occurred to him, but with a jolt of fear he blocked it out. It was time to escape; he was trespassing. He knelt for the dog, but the moment he touched it, it shot out of his hands, barking loudly.

The music stopped.

Heads turned.

Max froze, still kneeling.

A long silence.

Then all at once the musicians smiled—just about the friendliest smiles he had ever seen in his life.

"Why, you're not my grandson," the old man said, setting aside his wooden bass. "What can I do for you?"

Max, too afraid to speak, rose and looked at the dog.

"He belongs to you?" the old man asked.

Max nodded.

"We had a feeling you'd turn up. Name's George Addison. Everybody calls me Grampy. This here's my son Lewis."

The bald man with the trumpet tipped an invisible cap.

Grampy pointed: "That vision of loveliness, tickling the ivories, is his wife Lizzie."

"Welcome," Lizzie said, neatening her sheet music.

"And last but not least, manning the licorice stick is my grandson Bobby. His twin brother Billy plays the trombone, but he hasn't come home yet."

"You wanna go outside and play marbles?" Bobby asked Max. "Can we, Pop? I'm sick of practicing."

"Maybe in a little while," his father Lewis said, packing away his trumpet. "First we've got business to attend to." He smiled at Max. "You say the little terrier is yours, son?"

Max nodded.

"We didn't know what to call him, so we named him Fala."

Amused by the confusion on Max's face, Bobby explained, "You know, like the president's dog."

"Teatime!" Lizzie announced, rising from the bench.

"It's what separates man from beast," Grampy said to Max, with a wink.

Lizzie gave Max a maternal pat on the shoulder. "I do hope you'll join us."

Unloading groceries, Caroline tried desperately to think of something to say to her daughter, who stood at the kitchen counter, stone-faced, making herself a peanut-butter-and-jelly sandwich. Sally used to come home from school bursting with stories, but now that she was fourteen, she was mostly silent, offering only an occasional eye roll.

"Don't you want milk with that?" Caroline asked.

"No, thanks."

"I've got a fresh half-gallon of two percent."

"No, thanks."

"You don't want the peanut butter to stick to the roof of your mouth, do you?"

"Mother, please stop. Your happy homemaker act is revolting."

"What do you mean?"

"I mean it's the twenty-first century. Women don't have to pretend to like housework."

"Jim doesn't want me to find a job yet. He likes coming home to a hot meal."

"He's a savage. Who the hell cares what he wants?"

"I do!" Caroline cried out. "Maybe you think it's easy for a single mom to find a husband, but, let me tell you, it's not. I know plenty of women who'd kill to trade places with me."

Sally smirked skeptically. "Women who have actually *met* Jim?"

Caroline looked like she might cry. The wall phone rang. She grabbed the receiver, hand trembling. "Hello? Oh, yes. Hi, how are you?"

Perhaps sensing something, Sally did not escape, as

usual, to her bedroom. Instead, she sat down at the table with her sandwich, opened her book, and began to read. Her mother listened to the caller for a full minute without saying a word. Sally could hear that the caller was a woman, speaking with some urgency. Sally dared a glance. Her mother looked scared to death.

At last Caroline spoke: "But he's such a good student. And so well behaved. He never causes us any trouble. I just think—"

The lady interrupted and talked a while longer.

"Well, if you think so," Caroline said finally. "Okay then. Good-bye. Thank you so much."

After hanging up, Caroline thought for a while, then smiled uneasily at Sally, who was pretending to be engrossed in her book. "Max's social studies teacher wants him to see the school psychiatrist. She thinks his problems might be serious. A sensory disorder or something."

Sally shrugged her shoulders as though she couldn't have cared less, but her heart was racing. She adored Max just the way he was. She didn't like the idea of doctors poking around in his skull. Who knew what they might find.

As the sun sank over the distant trees and rooftops, a passing stranger glancing at the Addison house would have seen only a deserted ruin, never imagining that at that very moment a nine-year-old boy sat inside, cozy by a crackling fire, sipping a mug of peppermint tea.

Lewis smiled fondly at Max. "You know, son, if you don't start talkin' pretty soon, we're gonna think you don't like us."

"You haven't even told us your name yet," Bobby said.

Embarrassed, Max looked down at his cup. He *did* like them. They were the nicest people he had ever met. He closed his eyes, took a deep breath, and whispered, "Maxwell Thomas Beatty."

"A fine, triple-barreled name!" Grampy declared. "Well worth the wait."

Lizzie entered with a silver tray. "Raisin Molasses Pinwheels. Fresh from the oven."

The rich, syrupy smell made Max's stomach vibrate.

"Better move fast," Bobby warned him. "They won't last long with Grampy around."

Sure enough, the instant the tray hit the table, Grampy was already scooping four into a cloth napkin. Max struck like lightning and grabbed two for himself.

"Billy'll sure be sorry he missed these," Lizzie said. "Where do you suppose your fool brother's run off to?"

Bobby, cramming two cookies into his mouth, didn't even bother to answer.

Seated at the head of the dinner table, Jim pointed his beer bottle at his son. "Go ahead, Paulie. Tell 'em what we saw today."

"A house," Paul answered.

"Tell them how big it was."

"Big."

"And the land?"

"Also big."

"I can just picture it," Sally muttered dryly.

Jim's bushy eyebrows came together like two caterpillars. He banged a fist on the table near Paul, rattling the silverware. "You don't give a damn about anything!"

"Just me," Angela said with a smile, trying to lighten the mood.

"Well, he sure has a funny way of showing it."

"What do you mean?"

Now Jim pointed the bottle at her. "It means if he loved you, he'd wanna take care of you. You think he'll ever make a dime from that noise of his?"

"Well, first of all, it's not his noise. It's *our* noise. Second, he doesn't have to take care of me. I've worked since I was fourteen. In fact, I was just tired today at a diner downtown. And, third, yes, I do think our band will earn money someday."

"And the minute we do, we're outta here," Paul added.

Caroline, overhearing the argument and desperate for it to end, burst through the swinging door, carrying a tray of sizzling beef. "Ta-daaa!"

Jim beamed with pride. "Naughty girl. Did you dip into your cookie jar again?"

He liked to pretend that Caroline kept the insurance money she'd received from her husband's death in a cookie jar, when, in fact, like any sensible adult, she kept it in the bank.

As Jim set to carving the roast, Angela looked around the table. "Hey, where's Max?"

"Not home yet," Caroline said. "He probably stopped off at the library."

"But it's dark out."

Angela looked from face to face. No one seemed even remotely worried.

After spending just a few hours with the Addisons, Max already knew he would never find Fala a better home than this one, and so, when he rose to leave, he didn't even mention taking him. He had a feeling no one would notice, and he was right. At the front door everyone gathered around to say good-bye.

"Such a pleasure to meet you, Max," Lizzie said.

"Hope your folks aren't sore we kept you so long," said Grampy.

Bobby grinned. "Next time we'll play marbles."

Lewis helped him zip up his jacket. "You're always welcome here, son."

Max's face tingled at the touch of his strong hands. He remembered his father and all the little ways he had made him feel safe and cared for. Feeling a sob rise in his throat, Max turned quickly away, but, before he could exit, Lewis pressed something into his palm. Max looked down: the last cookie, the one everyone had been too polite to take for himself.

"Better skedaddle," Lewis said.

Max smiled and plunged into the cold night.

As he dashed across the front porch, he heard the door close behind him. He jumped all the way to the ground and ran. When he reached the sidewalk, he looked up at the vast autumn sky, pin-pricked with stars, and, feeling a rare surge of happiness, he spun around for one last wave good-bye to his new friends.

He couldn't believe it.

The house sat dark and dead. All the windows were either shuttered or black with soot. Even more impossible, the front door, through which he had just passed, was boarded up with dirty, old planks. Panicking, Max reached into his pocket and frantically searched. The cookie was gone.

Max ran as fast as he could. His mother had always said that if anything bad happened, he should never keep it a secret, that she would never punish him for telling the truth. But how do you tell your mother you're going insane? When he reached his front door, he heard Jim and Paul shouting at each other inside. He couldn't bear another fight—not after spending time with a family that was actually nice to each other. He silently turned the knob. He would go straight to his room.

Inside, he heard Paul say, "Angie's got a friend in Chicago named Tony Cermak."

"He's actually my uncle's friend," Angela said. "He books musicians all over the Midwest. I sent him our demo this morning. If he likes our stuff, do you know what that means?"

"He's tone deaf?" Jim said.

"God, you suck," Paul said.

"It was a joke, for Christ's sake! Why's everybody so touchy around here?"

Max tiptoed to the stairs, but the smell of roast beef stopped him. All he had eaten since school were two cookies, and they were probably not even real. He had no choice but to face his family.

When Max entered the dining room, Jim crooned: "Well, hello, little man!"

"Where'd you run off to?" Paul asked curiously.

"I was worried sick!" said Caroline.

"It's Mom's yummiest dinner ever," chimed Sally.

Spooked, Max recoiled, eyes wide.

Who *were* these people?

Then in a violent flash, his fantasy ended.

Jim was screaming at Paul: "Because that's what fathers do! We lecture! You don't like it, move the hell out!"

"Please stop fighting!" Caroline begged.

"Always such a delight to break bread with you all," Sally muttered.

"How dare you talk about hard work!" Paul yelled.

"All you do is think up get-rich-quick schemes that never come true!"

Jim rose from his chair, the veins bulging in his forehead, his huge frame blocking the light. "Shut up! Or I'll rip your god damn head off!"

Suddenly, Max heard himself screaming at the top of his lungs: *"Don't do it! Leave him alone! Leave him alone!"*

Every head turned and saw Max standing in the doorway—his face red, his jaw clenched, and his body rigid. Max couldn't believe it. Those words had actually come out of his mouth!

Jim looked rattled.

"Oh, baby," Caroline said, rising from her chair.

Max burst into tears and fled the room.

Angela rose, too, her eyes flashing at Jim. "You're a bully, you know that?"

Before Caroline could move, Angela hurried out of the room after Max.

Jim glanced a bit sheepishly from his wife to his son.

"So he's crying. Big deal. Kid's scared of his own shadow."

5.

EVEN THOUGH EVERYONE KNEW how hard Dr. Corwin worked to help kids solve their problems and overcome their obstacles, it didn't stop them from making fun of his impossibly hairy ears. Max had once drawn the good doctor's face with giant gray tarantulas crawling out of both earholes, and it wasn't much of an exaggeration. Today, however, sitting against his will in Corwin's office, Max sketched something else with the pencil and notepad the doctor had given him the moment he'd sat down.

"I can't help you if you won't talk," Dr. Corwin said, studying Max's sad eyes and determined little face. "Do me a favor. Say something, *anything*, before our time's up. Just so I can feel like we got something accomplished."

Max did not react.

It was though he had not even heard him.

Dr. Corwin made a sour face and began to scratch at a mustard stain on his red knit tie. "Miss Roland tells me that, aside from class participation, you're her top student. What do you like so much about Social Studies?"

Max did not look up, but, out of nowhere it seemed, he spoke—his words clear, almost confident. "I like to know what really happened."

It was the first time Dr. Corwin had ever heard Max speak. Encouraged, he reached across the desk. "Can I see it?"

Startled, Max slapped the notebook shut.

"Oops, sorry," the doctor said. "My bad. It's just that I'm excited to see your work."

Max stared at him. His teeth were yellow, his head was bald and shiny, and his ears looked extra hairy today, but Max knew if he was going to share his secret with anyone (and eventually he must), it made sense to tell someone whose actual job it was to help students with their problems. Also, he was fairly certain it was illegal for psychiatrists to tell anyone about their private conversations with patients. Or was that only with adult patients? He wasn't sure. Max took a deep breath, flipped opened the pad, and held it up for the doctor to see.

"Ew, scary," the doctor said, making a funny face.

"Only on the outside" Max explained. "Inside it's nice."

"How do you know?"

"I've been there."

"It's a real house?"

"Uh-huh."

"When were you inside it?"

"Yesterday after school. The day before, I chased a

dog inside. It had a broken leg, so I went back to try to help it."

"What happened?"

"The people who live there helped the dog. I'm not sure how they did it, but his leg wasn't broken anymore."

"Who are these people exactly?"

"A family. They play musical instruments. We had afternoon tea. It's what separates men from beasts."

Dr. Corwin frowned, confused. "Do these people have names?"

"The Addisons. The parents are Lewis and Lizzie. They have two kids. Bobby and Billy. I've only met Bobby. The grandfather's name is George. Everybody calls him Grampy."

"And you chased an injured dog into their house?"

"Yeah, the Addisons fixed his leg and named him Fala. Like the Scottish terrier that belonged to Franklin Delano Roosevelt, who was the American president during the Great Depression. It was a sad time in history, when everybody was poor, and all they had was each other."

Doctor Corwin's face went utterly blank.

The final bell rang.

Max wanted to tell him how the house looked burned from the outside but was perfect on the inside, and how a cookie that was real inside the house disappeared as soon as you stepped outside, but Dr. Corwin was writing so fast in his notebook that Max decided to save the rest for next time.

Crammed into a plaid suit two sizes too small, Jim Jarvis moved down the long central hallway of a retirement home. At his side, a huge, red-haired janitor pushed a squeaky cart of cleaning supplies. His fat, freckled arms were covered with tattoos. The men stopped at a pair of glass doors, through which elderly residents were visible, playing cards and games, watching TV, reading books, and tapping on their laptops.

"The old buzzard by the window," said the janitor.

Jim leaned closer and squinted. "Jesus, he looks like he's been dead a year."

"Pushing ninety."

"He got all his marbles?"

"Smarter than you and me put together."

Jim straightened his tie and grinned. "How do I look?"

"Like a guy who owes me a favor."

Jim laughed and opened one of the doors.

Ignoring the curious looks he received, Jim strode straight across the room to the old man, who sat in an armchair, reading a hardcover book. His posture was erect. A polished wooden cane leaned between his legs. Jim made his voice as soft and humble as possible. "Mr. Monroe?"

The man looked up curiously from his reading. Jim towered above him. "Yes?"

"Are you the owner of the house at 2453 Arcadia Lane?"

"I am."

"I got your name from hall of records, sir. I love your home, and I was wondering if by any chance you might be interested in selling it."

Monroe's brow tightened. He set aside his book. "Please sit down."

Jim lowered his big body into a matching armchair. A puff of dust rose.

"I didn't catch your name," Monroe said.

"James A. Jarvis, sir. People call me Jim."

"Mr. Jarvis, do you know that in all the years I've owned the house, I've never once considered selling it, till just a few days ago. Sitting right where you are now, my attorney said to me, 'You love the place so much, why leave it to *me* to sell? Sell it yourself, right now, to just the right buyer.' I saw his logic and I agreed. And now, like magic, you appear before me. It's uncanny."

"I'll say. Because I've had my eye on it for years, but never once thought of asking if it was for sale till just this morning. The time felt right somehow."

Monroe shook his head and repeated, "Uncanny."

"I'm not a rich man, sir. I don't wanna waste your time. Think you could give me some idea of the price?"

Monroe looked out the window. A passing police car stirred up a little tornado of dead leaves. "Money's got nothing to do with it. I don't have children. No family of any kind. My estate will go to the town library when I die. When it comes to the property, what I care about most is that I leave it in good hands. Someone who'll cherish it as much as I do."

"Of course," Jim said.

Monroe laid his shiny cane across his lap. "Tell me about yourself. Are you a married man?"

"I sure am. Tied the knot last August."

A shadow seemed to fall across Monroe's face. Realizing that this was perhaps not the answer the old man had been looking for, Jim started over: "You see, sir, for twelve years, my best friend, Tom Beatty, and I . . . we owned a little construction company over in Waterville called Top Tier Homes. We made a good living doing remodels. Then . . . about a year ago . . . there was a tragedy. Tom was visiting one of our sites on Eagle Lake. It was late. He'd had a few drinks. He slipped off the dock, hit his head, and drowned. Maybe you read about it in the papers?"

"I did, as a matter of fact. Heartbreaking."

"You have no idea. Barely forty years old. Left a wife and two kids behind. But I'd been left, too, you see. The summer before, my wife fell in love with a man she met on the Internet. A dentist. She moved down to Florida to be with him. Left me to raise our son alone. In the beginning, I helped out Tom's widow—Caroline's her name—in little ways. I bought her groceries, mowed the lawn, patched the roof, things like that. Every couple of weeks, I'd take her and her kids out to dinner and a movie. Gradually, I became sort of a second father to Sally and little Max. And as for Caroline, well, we fell in love." Tears welled in Jim's narrow eyes. "I don't want the house for myself, Mr. Monroe. I want it for Caroline and the kids. And for my boy Paul. A place where two families can become one."

After school, when Max arrived at the Addisons' back door, he wasn't sure what he would find inside. The vanishing cookie had forced him to question everything that had happened the afternoon before. Before entering, he drew as deep a breath as he could, and held it. He was thrilled to see that everything was just as he had discovered it the day before, except Lizzie stood at the counter now, flattening a blob of dough with a rolling pin.

"Well, hello, Max. How are you?"

"Fine, Mrs. Addison. How are you?" Max marveled at how easy it was to speak inside the house. He wasn't frightened at all.

"Oh, no complaints," Lizzie replied. "Go on inside. We're all gathered in the parlor."

Max moved to the swinging door, but Lizzie stopped him.

"Is Billy out in the yard?"

"I don't think so," Max replied. "What does he look like?"

"Same as Bobby. They're twins."

"Oh, right. No, ma'am, I didn't."

She shook her head, muttering, "Where do you suppose that little rascal ran off to?"

Max moved through the house and arrived in the parlor just as practice was beginning. Bobby was twisting together his clarinet. Lewis made popping sounds with his trumpet. Grampy slid his bow across a lump of what looked like dried honey.

"Maxwell!" Grampy said. "Right on time. I'm just giving the old horsetail some rosin. Let's get you started."

"Horsetail?"

Ignoring the question, Grampy set down his bow and led Max to a tall oak cabinet. He swung open double doors to reveal an assortment of musical instruments lying on shelves and hanging off hooks.

"Go ahead. Pick one."

Max looked at him as though he were crazy.

"Take your time," Grampy cautioned, "because it could turn out to be your best friend. Sweethearts come and go, empires rise and fall, but a musical instrument is true blue forever."

"Anything catch your eye?" Lewis asked, appearing behind Max and laying a hand on his shoulder.

Max studied the instruments: flute, trombone, saxophone, triangle, xylophone . . . .

Finally he pointed.

"Splendid choice," Lewis declared. "The alto sax."

"Awful big horn for a little fella," Grampy said as he

took it down from its hook.

"It'll sound swell with Billy's trombone," Bobby said.

Grampy carefully screwed a thin strip of wood into the mouthpiece, then handed the horn to Lewis, who, after adjusting the leather strap, lowered it over Max's head.

"Feel about right?"

Max nodded uncertainly.

"Okay, lick the reed," Lewis said, pointing to the wood.

Max stared at it, then flicked his tongue, like a lizard gathering raindrops.

"No, get it good and spitty. Slobber it up!"

Obeying, Max laid down a big glob of saliva.

"Now mush it around. There you go. Perfect. Now look at my mouth. See my lips and tongue? It's what's called your *embouchure*. Fancy French word. Make it nice and tight. Like this. Try it. Good. Now give it a blow."

Max, imitating Lewis as best he could, inhaled and blew hard. A tiny squeak. Fala cocked his head on the window seat.

"Not bad," said Lewis. "Try it again."

This time Max's mighty effort produced a small honk.

"Bravo," Lizzie said, entering with a tray of lemonade.

Grampy pointed to the window. "Stand over there, kid. When you feel like joining in, just blow. Whatever comes out, that's what's known as 'music.'"

Max found it hard to believe that playing an

instrument could possibly be this easy, but he was happy to go along with it.

When the front door slammed, Caroline's heart stirred with excitement as it always did when her husband returned home.

"Whatever you're cooking, sure smells good," Jim said, walking into the dining room, rubbing his big hands together.

"Can you guess?" she asked, setting down a dinner plate.

"Steak?"

"Nope. Too chewy. He might wear false teeth."

"Good thinking."

Caroline blushed at the compliment. Jim wrapped his arms around her and gave her a peck on the lips, making her blush even redder.

"Some sorta fish?" he guessed.

"Nope, bones. He could choke."

"More good thinking. I give up."

"Meatloaf, roasted potatoes, and green salad. Comfort food. And I baked an apple pie."

"Baby, you're a genius. Can't get any more all-American than that. Where're the kids?"

"Sally's in her room, getting all dolled up."

"She'd better be. For what I'm paying her. How about the others?"

Jim got his answer with a burst of music from below. He stomped his boot and shouted at the floor. "Let's clear it out! Right now! Half-hour till showtime!"

In the basement, Paul smirked apologetically at the Fosters, two gangly brothers with long blond hair and sweatshirts without sleeves. One sat at a drum set, the other held a guitar.

"Sorry, guys. Angela and I got an acting gig. We gotta pretend we can stand my dad's guts. If we pull it off, we get two hundred bucks each."

"And lose our souls," Angela sighed, switching off her microphone.

Upstairs, Jim clapped his hands and cheered as Sally descended from the second floor, smiling falsely and waving a stiff hand like a beauty pageant contestant. She wore the same puffy, green dress she had been forced to wear to her cousin's wedding.

"Perfect," Jim said. "Where's the midget?"

"Not home yet."

"Good."

"Whatcha waitin' for?" Grampy shouted above the music.

"Join in!" Lewis said.

"Don't be afraid!" said Lizzie.

"Just blow!" Bobby cried.

Max sucked in as much air as he could, wedged the

reed between his pursed lips, and blew mightily. His cheeks ballooned, his eyes bulged, and his butt erupted with a loud honk. Fala jumped off the sofa and barked at him. Everyone stopped playing. Max expected mockery. Instead, everybody laughed as though it were the most wonderful thing imaginable.

"A whopper!" said Bobby.

"Occupational hazard!" Grampy warned.

"Out with the bad, in with the good," said Lewis.

"Give it another try," Lizzie instructed as she began to play the piano again.

Max inhaled deeply and blew again. The sax squawked.

"Now you're gettin' it!" Grampy said.

"Keep the lips nice and tight," Lewis reminded him.

Gaining confidence, Max began emitting little squawks and pops and beeps in time to the song. The Addisons could not have seemed more pleased if he had actually known what he was doing. Soon, much to his own surprise, Max began to experience that he *did* know what he was doing and that perhaps this was some sort of music after all.

Despite being squeezed together around the small table, dinner was coming off splendidly. Three times Mr. Monroe had complimented Caroline on her cooking, and he seemed utterly delighted by Sally, Paul, and Angela, who, impeccably dressed and groomed, came off as sterling examples of well-mannered youth.

"Paulie here is a musician," said Jim. "Classically trained."

"Angela and I are part of a string quartet," Paul offered. "We perform the works of the famous Austrian composer, Joseph Haydn.

"We call it 'Haydn Go Seek,'" Angela added. "We hope to go on tour soon. Mostly local schools and churches."

The whole thing was so ridiculous that it was a wonder they could keep a straight face.

"The ability to make music is truly a blessing, isn't it?" Monroe said, lifting his glass of cider.

"Yes, sir, it is," Paul replied. "And a privilege."

Jim pointed with his knife. "Sally here's the egghead of the family. Top of her class. Always got her nose in a book."

Monroe was delighted. "Is that so?"

"Yes, sir, I'm a hopeless bibliophile. If I had my way, I'd be married to a poem and given away by a novel." She smiled like an angel and sipped her water.

Caroline offered Monroe a platter of roasted potatoes. "Would you like some more, Mr. Monroe?"

"Oh, no, thank you. I'm still working on my seconds. They're delicious."

"I hope the meatloaf isn't too chewy." Caroline touched her lips. "In case you wear false—"

Jim bulged his eyes at her, which immediately shut her up.

"My teeth are all my own, I'm proud to report." Monroe smiled at Jim and pointed a long, shaky finger. "I notice we have an empty chair."

"What? Oh, yeah. Max. He . . . uhhh . . . well, he's not home from school yet."

Monroe looked slightly alarmed. "So late?"

Sally came to the rescue: "Practice must have run overtime. He's on the debate team."

Paul laughed, but covered it with a fast cough.

In the next room, a door opened and closed. Anxious glances darted around the table. Max had not been briefed on the evening's make-believe. Cash prizes were at stake here. Luckily, Max hardly ever spoke, so the odds were slim to none that he could do any serious damage.

6.

WHEN MAX STEPPED INTO the dining room and saw his family, well-dressed and cheerful, sitting around the table grinning at him, he looked away, certain that when he looked back, they would return to their warring natural state. But instead their smiles only grew brighter. Afraid and confused, Max walked slowly towards the only empty chair. From amid the chorus of warm greetings, a deep, male voice emerged: "How was debate practice?"

Max looked.

At the end of the table sat the old man who had handed him the book at the library. How was this possible? Max quickly closed his eyes and opened them again. The man was still there. He was real.

"Upsy-daisy!" Jim wrenched Max off his feet and dropped him into his chair.

"Max, meet our special guest," Caroline said. "Mr. Monroe."

"Actually, we've met before," the old man said. "Just last week. At the public library."

"Small world," Jim said, sounding a little bit nervous.

"Positively claustrophobic," marveled Sally.

"Eat up, little man. It's your favorite." Caroline laid a plate down in front of him.

With no idea what was going on, Max lowered his head and began to eat. After everyone had a good laugh at the ferocity of his appetite, the conversation picked up just where it had left off: Monroe making every effort to get to know the family, and the family making every effort to make sure that he did not. Max had no idea why they would want to deceive such a nice, old man, but sensing that it was none of his business, he stayed out of it.

After everyone had finished eating, Caroline said, "Shall we retire to the living room for some apple pie à la mode?"

Max had never heard his mother use the words "shall" and "retire" before, and she had certainly never spoken French. Just as strange, she was wearing her grandmother's pearl necklace, which was normally reserved for weddings and funerals.

In the living room, Jim knelt down at the hearth, where three logs smoked over a bed of burning magazines and newspaper. It was the first time since moving that they had used the fireplace. Caroline offered Monroe the most comfortable chair in the room. With the help of his cane, Monroe sank into its feathery cushions with a look of obvious pleasure.

During dessert, Jim began to brag about what a

good little ball player his stepson was. "Yup, Maxie came through with the winning home run in last year's city championship. They gave him an MVP trophy taller than he was."

In fact, Max was hopelessly, embarrassingly, ambidextrous. The first time he had ever played baseball, in kindergarten, he had stood with both feet on home plate, facing the pitcher and pointing the bat at him, having no idea which way to turn. The other kids laughed so hard that he had never picked up a bat again. He always got a C in gym. Why did Jim want Mr. Monroe to think he was good at sports? Wasn't it enough that he got A's in everything else?

After the dishes were cleared, Monroe glanced at his gold wristwatch. "Well, I suppose we'd better get down to business."

Jim jumped to his feet and told the kids to clear out. Thrilled to be finished with the charade, Sally, Paul, and Angela said good night and practically ran for the stairs. Max, sensing that the mystery of the evening was about to be revealed, decided to stay put.

"Come on, kiddo," Jim said. With a forced laugh, he yanked Max to his feet and gave him a smack on the butt so hard it practically knocked him to the floor.

"Good night, Max," Monroe said.

Max trudged upstairs in silence.

The moment he was out of sight, however, he turned around and sat on a step.

He listened, ears pricked, like a spy.

"I dreaded the idea of hiring a real estate broker," Monroe explained. "People traipsing in and out of my house all day. Caroline, you've seen the place, I trust."

Jim jumped in before she could answer: "You bet she has. She's in love with it. 'A dream come true,' she called it."

Pleased, Monroe continued: "As I'm sure you noticed, it caught fire a long time ago. The structure's sound, but it'll take a lot of hard work to restore it to its original beauty."

"I told her that," Jim replied. "And do you know what she said? 'When it's for your family, nothing's impossible.' That's why I married her, sir. She's one in a million."

Max's mouth fell open. It all made sense now. Monroe owned the Addisons' house. Now that he was old, he wanted to sell it to someone who would take good care of it. Since Jim just wanted to chop it up for money, Jim knew the only way he could get Monroe to sell it to him was to pretend it was for his family to live in.

Thinking fast, Max rose, tiptoed down the stairs, and ran silently to the front door. He ducked behind a coat rack, heart pounding. No one had spotted him. He grabbed a jacket off a hook and made for the door.

A half-hour later, Monroe sat in the passenger seat of Jim's car as it glided down a dark residential street. "I'm told the land alone is worth well over a hundred thousand dollars. And the same goes for the house."

"That's a lot of money," Jim said uneasily.

"Jim, I told you money is the least of my concerns, and I meant it. The house needs a family, and your family needs a home. What would you say to a hundred thousand dollars for the house *and* the land? Might you be able to manage that?"

"I . . . I think I could, sir," Jim said, genuinely stunned.

"Well, then we have a deal."

Jim parked in front of the Oakview Retirement Home, his face red, as though he had just run a mile. "I want to thank you for your generosity, sir. I won't let you down. Thank you!"

He vigorously shook the old man's hand.

"You're more than welcome," Monroe said. "You'll take care of the paperwork?"

"You bet."

"Keep it simple. No escrow. No fuss."

"You got it. Here, let me help you out."

"Unnecessary." Monroe opened the door himself, and, with a slight grunt and the help of his cane, made it to his feet.

As Monroe walked away, Jim sat motionless, growling to himself: "Finally . . . finally . . . finally . . . some *luck!*"

Jim's moment of triumph was cut short, however, by a breeze tickling his neck. He stretched across for the passenger door, assuming Monroe hadn't closed it properly, but was confused to see that he had. He whipped around and looked over his shoulder. One of the back doors was open.

At that moment, just as Monroe was about to open the door to the retirement home, he felt a tug on his sleeve. The last thing he expected to see were Max's big brown eyes looking up at him.

"What on earth—"

"You can't sell him your house!" Max blurted, his breath cloudy in the cold air.

"Why not?"

"People live inside it. Jim doesn't love it. He just wants to—"

The slap of Jim's heavy boots on the pavement stopped him like a hand around the throat. Max whipped around in fear.

"Little rascal was hiding in the back seat the whole time," Jim said. "Come on. Bedtime."

Monroe smiled quizzically. "He doesn't think I should sell you my house."

"What?" Jim laughed.

"Tell me why," Monroe asked Max.

Max wanted desperately to answer, but Jim's huge hand was on the back of his neck, gently squeezing.

"*I* know why," Jim said. "The kid hates change. It's to be expected, I guess, given what happened with his dad and all. He still throws a fit every time his mom changes the sheets on his bed. He wants to wear the same thing to school every day. And don't get me started on the treatment I got after she told him we were getting married."

Monroe looked down at Max. "I know it's scary, but I'm afraid change is all we poor mortals have. Life's nothing *but* change. All you can do is accept it. Maybe even learn to enjoy it a little bit. You'll be happy in the house, I promise."

Monroe turned around and went inside.

Jim walked Max back to the car, his hand still clamped to the back of his neck.

"What's the matter with you?" he spit between clenched teeth.

Later, lying in the dark, listening to the autumn wind rattle the window above his radiator, Max felt like the loneliest human on earth. At some point he must have fallen asleep, because the next thing he knew his eyes were open and there were shouts coming from behind the wall by his head. At first he thought Jim was drunk and angry, but then he realized that he was drunk and *happy*.

"My whole life it was the other guy who got the breaks. Well, not anymore! A house that big for a hundred thousand? After the remodel, it'll be worth three times that. We're rich, baby!"

"Where're you gonna get the down payment?" she asked. "Do you need some help? I could chip in."

"You think I'd let you dip into your cookie jar for me? Never!"

"But then how—"

"The bank. It'll be a cinch to get a loan. Come here, pretty girl. Give your big man some love."

Max rolled onto his side and squeezed his pillow over his ear. There was so much about the situation he didn't understand, but he knew one thing for sure: Jim had to be stopped.

7.

GRAMPY CREAKED in his rocking chair by the fire, holding Fala and listening to laughter on the radio. On the sofa, Lewis read the newspaper while Lizzie knitted a scarf by his side. Bobby lay on the floor, examining pennies through a large magnifying glass. Max, having arrived unnoticed in the archway, was too embarrassed to intrude on their contentment. As he turned to leave, Lizzie looked up.

"Well, look who's here!"

"Maxie! Sit right down. Make yourself at home," Lewis said.

"Want to see my Indian Heads?" Bobby asked.

Max didn't move or speak.

"Cat got your tongue?" Grampy asked. "If he did, just say the word, and we'll set Fala on 'im."

Everyone laughed but Max.

Lewis scooted over a couple of feet and patted the fat cushion. "Come on, sit down."

Max timidly obeyed.

Lizzie laid a hand on his shoulder. "What's the matter? Are you blue?"

Unused to being asked how he felt about anything, Max blinked back tears.

"Did something happen, son?" Lewis asked.

Max nodded.

"If you clam up about it," Grampy said, "it only gets worse. Didn't you know that?"

Max did *not* know that, but it made sense. He never talked about his problems, and they never got better.

Max took a deep breath. "My stepfather's going to buy your house."

The Addisons glanced among each other.

"And how's he going to manage that," Lewis asked, "when it's not for sale?"

"It *is* for sale," Max said. "An old man owns it. His name's Mr. Monroe. Do you know him?"

They all shook their heads.

"He's really old and wants to sell it to someone who's gonna fix it up nice. He thinks my stepdad Jim wants it for our family to live in, but Jim really just wants to carve it up."

Bobby screwed up his face. "Like a pumpkin?"

"Yeah, so he can flip it."

"Flip it?"

"Make it into apartments and sell them off. Then with the money he makes, he'll buy another old house to carve up. He thinks it's the quickest way to get rich. He thinks he has vision and can see the future."

Lewis's smile was patient. "It doesn't matter what he

thinks, Max. Or what his plans are. I own this place free and clear, and it's not, and never will be, for sale."

Max started to speak again but caught himself.

"Say it," Lizzie instructed. "Whatever's on your mind."

"Are you *ghosts?*" Max blurted.

Grampy's laughter was so high-pitched that Fala jumped off his lap and skittered across the polished floor.

"Well, I never," Lizzie said, shaking her head.

Bobby was indignant. "What the heck kinda question is that?"

"But real people have jobs," Max insisted. "They go to school. Leave the house sometimes."

Everyone smiled at him, shaking their heads, as though he though he were the funniest, silliest boy.

A chill ran through Max. What if *he* was the ghost? That's how it had felt since his father died. As though life were just one long dream he couldn't wake up from. Or like a sad story happening to somebody else.

"I don't know anything anymore," Max confessed at last.

Lewis, cleaning his eyeglasses with a handkerchief, considered Max's situation. "When you aren't too sure what the truth is, I guess the best you can do is figure out your *own* truth and stand by it, come what may."

Max looked at him and slowly nodded.

Crammed again into the same plaid suit, Jim poked at his oily hair in the car's rear-view mirror. "This could take a while. You know how it is with banks and loans. They ask you a million dumb-ass questions, then bury you in paper."

Paul, sitting behind the steering wheel, did not reply. He had no idea what banks did or did not do, and he couldn't have cared less.

Jim returned the mirror to its correct position and handed his son a ten-dollar bill. "Buy yourself a cheeseburger. I'll call you when I'm out. Wish me luck."

"Good luck," Paul said flatly.

"Thanks."

Jim jumped out. Looming above him was the tallest and oldest building in town—the Union County Savings Bank. He straightened his tie, blasted his tongue with peppermint spray, then, pasting on his most convincing smile, strode toward the bank's four stately columns. When he reached the entrance, he glanced over his shoulder and saw that Paul was still there, texting someone. He watched as Paul dropped his phone on the seat and pulled into traffic.

As the car drove past him, Jim smiled, waved, and plunged into one of the bank's revolving doors. It spun and spun and a moment later delivered him back to the pavement, right where he had started. He looked up and down the block. No sign of anyone. Relaxing now, he walked away, whistling to himself, smiling in each shop window, like a man with all the time and money in the world.

At the corner, he stopped under a neon sign and yanked open an old-fashioned, etched-glass door. It was dark inside but for a few flashing televisions. He dropped onto the first stool, rapping his knuckles on the oak bar—a cocky rat-a-tat-tat.

The bartender walked over. "What can I get you?"

"Scotch. On the rocks. Make it a double."

"Startin' awful early."

"I'm celebrating," Jim said. "In advance."

Max entered the Oakview Retirement Home, expecting to be shooed away—or, much worse, thrown into a locked room until his mother came to pick him up. Instead, no one even noticed him—not the bored security guard painting her long, curved fingernails at the front desk or the janitor emptying a wastebasket into a bin on wheels. Sometimes it was a good thing to be invisible, Max thought, as he pushed through the swinging glass door.

He walked quickly down a carpeted hallway, past a cafeteria where an old man was banging his fist on a candy machine. Farther on, a tiny lady in a wheelchair prayed in front of burning candles and a plastic stained-glass window. At the end of the hall, he turned right at a brick wishing well and entered the part of the building where the old people actually lived. Most of the bedroom doors were left open, and he could see that they were all pretty much the same—a twin bed, brown curtains, and a TV.

"Max?"

Max spun around.

Mr. Monroe was bent over a drinking fountain. "What on earth are you doing here?"

"I need to talk to you," Max replied.

Monroe's face fell serious. "This way," he said, pointing with his cane. "After you."

Max pushed through the door into a large room, where old people were busy doing quiet things. Monroe caught up with him and led him to a little table at which a bald black man with a diamond earring was setting up chess pieces.

"Patrick," Monroe said, "I'm afraid our game will have to be postponed. My young friend here requires my full and immediate attention."

"Well, that's all right," the man said. "I'm not goin' anywhere and neither are you."

Both men laughed, as Monroe led Max to a couch and armchair by the window. Once Monroe had settled himself into the chair and Max onto the couch, he laid his cane across his lap and, with a tiny nod, said, "I'm all ears."

Max collected himself, determined not to leave anything out. He noticed a huge man with red hair mopping the floor nearby. He looked like he might be eavesdropping.

Max explained slowly: "The reason I don't want you to sell your house to Jim isn't because I hate change. It's because people live there."

"Inside my house?"

"Yes."

"Squatters?"

"What's that?"

"Homeless people in need of shelter."

"No, these people *own* the house."

"My house?"

"Yes."

"Of course not."

"They *say* they do."

"They're deceiving you."

"That's what they said about you."

"But I've owned it for almost eighty years now. Since I was your age."

"How can a kid own a house?"

The old man breathed heavily in and out, as adults do when they're about to share something difficult: "I was born in that house. It caught fire when I was ten years old. No one knows what started it. When I woke up, my bedroom was already thick with smoke. I escaped out my window. I slid down a gable onto the roof of the parlor. When I hit the front lawn, neighbors had already gathered there. The fire brigade was on its way, they said.

Everyone ran around, screaming the names of everyone trapped inside. Every time someone broke open a door or smashed a window, smoke poured out. It was impossible to get in. At one point, I thought I heard someone screaming inside, but I wasn't sure. I ran around to the backyard. The porch was thick with smoke. I tried to go in, but a big man lifted off my feet and held me while I kicked and hollered. By the time the fire brigade arrived, it was too late. No one made it out."

Monroe breathed for a few seconds, tears pooling in his milky, blue eyes. He cleared his throat and went on: "A few weeks after the funeral, a family over in Rock Creek adopted me. Eugene and Clara Monroe. Fine people, who provided for me in every way. They adopted me. Over the years, family and friends advised me to sell the house. Leave the past behind, they said. But I didn't want to forget. I wanted to remember my family for as long as I could. But now— Now, it doesn't really matter anymore. I'll be gone soon. I'll take my memories of my family with me. There won't be a single, living soul left on earth who ever knew them."

Max's eyes were filled with tears too now.

"What's your name?" he whispered.

"Pardon me?"

"Your first name."

"William."

Max's scalp tingled.

"Your family isn't dead, Billy."

The old man flinched, as though someone had jabbed him with a pin.

"Your family's in the house," Max said. "They're waiting for you to come home."

8.

"I HAVEN'T STEPPED FOOT inside since the fire," Monroe said, standing in the backyard of the house on Arcadia Lane. "I think I was afraid of what I might see."

"What do you mean?" Max asked.

"Some sign that my mother or father . . . or my brother . . . had woken up . . . tried to escape . . . and been trapped . . . suffered."

"It's not scary at all," Max said, taking Monroe's hand and pulling him forward. "Everybody's waiting for you. Watch what happens when I step on the porch!"

He walked the old man across a carpet of damp, dead leaves and laid his sneaker on the first step. The lights popped on and the music played. Max whipped his head around and grinned at Monroe, but his grin soon vanished when he saw the blank look on Monroe's face.

"Don't you hear it?"

"Hear what?"

"The music." Max ran over to the window. "The lights are on in the kitchen. See? Your family's practicing music in the parlor."

Monroe stared at him in mute confusion.

Max ran back to Monroe, took his hand again, and pulled. Monroe allowed himself to be led across the porch and through the open back door.

"See the kitchen?"

"Yes," Monroe whispered. "A burned, blackened ruin."

"No!" Max cried. "The curtains are yellow with little red flowers. The tablecloth's blue and white. Your mom makes raisin molasses pinwheel cookies. I had to move fast because of Grampy."

Before Monroe could respond, there was a bang. Max turned around, startled. The swinging door opened, and Fala pushed his way in. Tail wagging, he scampered over and jumped up to lick Max's face. Giggling happily, Max looked up at Monroe, and knew with a chill that all the old man could see was a little boy petting the air.

"Fala's right here," Max protested. "I swear it."

"Fala?"

"Your dog."

"But we never owned one."

Max was embarrassed by his mistake. "Oh, right. You weren't home when I chased him inside. You see— Oh, never mind. It doesn't matter. Come on!" Max swiftly grabbed Monroe's hand again and pulled him through the swinging door with Fala at their heels.

As they moved through the house, Max checked Monroe every few seconds for any sign of recognition, but his face showed only the pain of unwelcome memory.

Max tried to help him, pointing things out. "The grandfather clock is even taller than you are. It's got a smiling moon painted on it. And there's a metal eagle on top. What do you see?"

Monroe's eyes were moist. "What's left of it. It's mostly ashes now."

Max pointed out the crystal lamp that threw splashes of rainbow on the walls, and in the living room he led him to the old radio set in its glistening wood cabinet, but again Monroe saw none of it.

Finally, Max pointed at the coffee table. "Look, Bobby left out his Indian Head collection."

More afraid than amazed, Monroe cried out, "How could you possibly know about it? You must have seen a photograph."

"No, it's right there!" Desperate to the point of panic, Max ran to the parlor doors and beckoned Monroe, shouting above the musical racket inside: "Come here! Say hello!"

Max threw open the doors. His one last hope: even if Monroe couldn't see his family, maybe they could see him.

"There he is!" Grampy said, plucking the strings of his bass.

"Hello, stranger!" Lizzie said from the piano.

"Grab your horn," Lewis instructed.

"Look!" Max said. "It's Billy! I found him! He's home!"

The Addisons looked everywhere.

They were as confused as Monroe, who stood in the doorway now, bewildered.

"Where?" Bobby asked.

"Right here!" Max said, pointing at the ceiling. "His face is right here. He's really tall."

Bobby laughed. "Billy's the same height as me. He's three minutes older, but nobody can tell."

"No! He's an old man now," Max explained.

The family laughed.

"You been down to Casey's Pub?" Grampy asked.

Monroe stepped closer to Max and spoke firmly. "Time to go."

"Why? Your family's right here! Your mom tickles the ivories. Your dad plays the trumpet. Grampy plays the bass. Bobby plays the licorice stick. Your trombone's right there in that cabinet!"

Monroe's eyes blazed suddenly, and he shouted, *"No more!"*

Max stopped breathing.

Monroe, struggling to calm himself, laid both trembling hands on Max's shoulders. "I wish I could see them, but I can't. I need to go home now. Rest."

Max swallowed hard, his eyes welling with tears.

"Are you all right, dear?" Lizzie asked, rising from her bench.

Max whipped around and cried from the heart. "Everybody thinks I'm crazy, but I'm not!"

Max dashed for the door.

Monroe moved to follow him at the same moment that the Addisons did, but, knowing he would never catch up, Monroe stopped. When Max glanced over his shoulder to see if he was being followed, he saw the Addisons pass right through Mr. Monroe as though he were a ghost.

Max ran even faster now and burst out the back door as though fleeing for his life. Halfway across the yard, he spun his head around. The Addisons were bunched at the edge of the porch, as though it presented some sort of barrier beyond which they could not step. They called out his name, pleading with him to come back, but he banged through the gate into the alleyway without a word of good-bye.

Monroe, left alone in the parlor, studied the burned remnants of an Oriental carpet, the baked wallpaper blotched with water stains, a window seat reduced to cold, ragged ash. He turned a slow circle, remembering where each member of his family had stood when they made their music. He stopped abruptly and his eyes blossomed with pity. Behind the ruins of his mother's piano lay a little dog, curled into a ball, one of its hind legs bent awkwardly behind him. It had been dead for few days.

Caroline watched from the sofa as Jim paced the floor in his heavy boots, his cigarette trailing smoke.

"What the hell was I thinking?" he shouted. "Banks aren't charities! They don't *give* money away. Doesn't matter what you need it for . . . how great a deal you got lined up . . . they only lend you money if they know you're gonna pay it back, and they don't think I can. And why should they? My credit stinks!" He stopped and pulled at his own hair, punishing himself for his stupidity.

"Don't do that, baby," Caroline begged.

"My credit was always perfect! It's not my fault Tom died!"

"Of course not."

"I told the guy at the bank how hard it was to run the business without him. He didn't care. He just knows it went under. He's demanding a forty-percent down payment! Who ever heard of that? You should have seen the way he looked at me. Like I was dirt!"

"I'm so sorry."

"How am I going to come up with that kinda dough? I've got nothing to sell. The van's twelve years old. My car's even older. I got nothing!"

"You've got *me*. And I've got the cookie jar."

Jim turned around slowly, doing his best to look astonished. "You'd do that for me? You'd lend me the money?"

Her smile was sweet and trusting. "We're a team, right?"

Jim fell at her feet and hugged her knees. "Baby, thank you! I'll pay you back every penny!"

"How much do you need?"

"The sale price is a hundred thousand and another two-fifty to do the remodel. That's three-fifty total. Forty percent of that is a hundred and forty even."

"Well, I can't give you *that* much, but—"

Jim, still kneeling, grabbed her by the wrist, a little too tightly. "What do you mean?"

"I've only got thirty-eight thousand left. I could give you fifteen or twenty, I guess, but I need to keep something for us to live on till you're on your feet again."

"You cleared fifty thousand on the house. Tom's insurance was another two hundred. What the hell'd you do with it?"

"Well, there were bills to pay off. There was the funeral . . . the wedding . . . the move. Don't forget, I paid for pretty much everything. And . . . and then I put a hundred and twenty-five thousand in the kids' college fund. Maybe you could find an investor. A partner who—"

"No, I need that college money."

"I can't do that."

"Why not? You'll get it back."

Caroline's eyes widened with fear.

Jim's narrowed with suspicion. "You don't trust me?"

"Of course I do, but . . . but what if something happens?"

"Like what? What's gonna happen? I'll pay you back with interest."

"If the kids can't go to college—"

"What's mine is yours, and yours is mine, remember? That's what you said."

Still holding her by the wrist, he smiled faintly and began to ever so slowly twist it.

Max walked the streets for hours, through neighborhoods he had never seen before. Sometimes cars slowed down when they saw him, blinding him with their headlights. He prayed no one would stop and talk to him. He knew what he was doing was dangerous and that he would probably be punished when he got home, but he had to figure out what was happening to him. Yet no matter how many times he went over the facts, he always ended up at the same conclusion: The Addisons were definitely ghosts. Not just any ghosts. *Ghosts that only he could see.* But since he knew there was no such thing, he had no choice but to start all over again, turning the facts around and around in his head until he felt like he was about to faint. Finally, cold and famished, and feeling utterly defeated, he headed for home.

As he entered his house, Max heard Jim upstairs, screaming his head off. Hoping to slip into bed unnoticed, Max climbed the stairs as slowly and quietly as he could. Even though it meant going to sleep hungry, anything was better than being around Jim when he was drunk like this.

At the landing outside their door, he heard his mother pleading: "But in business things go wrong all the time. Things you can't control."

"So maybe your kids won't go to college! They'll get jobs and work their asses off like I did. It's not the end of the world." His voice was filled with scorn now. "You're just like your kids, you know that? Doubting me! Tearing me down. How do you think that feels?"

His mother started to sob.

Max wanted to go in and protect her, but he couldn't move. His feet felt bolted to the floor. His heart began to race. Pictures began to flash through his mind. Not daydreams, not fantasies. No, not this time. These visions were real and alive. These were memories. Ones that had always been there, just at the edge of his consciousness, but they emerged now, clear and sharp, as though just a few moments old, when, in fact, they were born almost a year before.

Eagle Lake. A big silver moon hangs over the water. Max, hiding, peers out from the open driver's window of his father's van. Jim's car, parked sideways, shines its headlights on an old wooden dock, where Jim and his father are in the middle of a terrible argument. His father is angrier than Max has ever seen him, pointing a finger in Jim's face and calling him a thief.

Finally, his father walks away, back towards Max. Max is relieved. Soon they will drive away and all will be well again. But then, without any warning, Jim runs up and punches his father on the side of the head, knocking him down. While he is still on his back, Jim kicks him in the ribs with his big boot. His father rolls off the dock into the water, but there's almost no splash because there are rocks. Jim, looking scared, jumps in and pulls him out, but blood drips from his father's head. Shocked, Jim drops him back.

When the memories ended, Max was still standing at the closed door, and Jim was still screaming his head off. A strange tingling traveled down Max's arms, like electricity leaving his body, making his hands tighten into claws. And then suddenly it left him, and he was free. He could move his fingers again. He banged his fists on the door and shouted louder than he had ever shouted in his life. *"Stop it! Don't hurt her! Or I'll call the police!"*

Silence.

Heavy footsteps.

The door flew opened.

Jim's smile was an ugly smear. "Well, look who's back. While I'm at the bank, begging for a loan, this little traitor's at the old folk's home, telling Monroe to back out of the deal."

"That isn't true," Caroline said.

Max leaned sideways until he could see her, behind Jim, sitting on the bed.

"Yes, it is," Max said. "He doesn't love the house. He just wants to carve it up for money."

Jim's eyes narrowed into slits. "And what if I do?

What's wrong with that? You don't like money? You wanna starve?"

Max backed away.

Jim lunged at him.

From out of nowhere, Sally stepped into his path.

"Out of my way!" Jim barked.

Sally's face showed no emotion at all. "What're you gonna do? Hit me? Go ahead. You lay a hand on me, they'll throw you in jail where you belong."

Jim's face turned red. His lip curled. Just when it seemed he might explode, Caroline got up from the bed, declaring softly, "Take the money."

Jim ever so slowly relaxed. He grinned at Sally. "Good night, little girl." He walked over and pulled Caroline into a tight hug. He stroked her thin, silky hair. "You're the best. We're gonna be rich, baby. You'll see.

Her voice was tiny. "Just pay me back, okay?"

"You bet," he muttered before kissing her.

Sally took Max by the hand and led him out of the room.

A minute later, Sally sat on the edge of Max's bed as he changed into his pajamas. "He's a monster," she said, almost matter-of-factly. "But he's part of our family now, and there's nothing we can do about it. We can't divorce him. Only Mom can. And she won't. For some reason, she thinks she needs him to survive. Which is beyond sad. Anyway, I guess what I'm saying is, just accept that he's gonna be around for a while and don't hope for the best. Hope makes everything hurt worse when nothing changes."

Max was surprised to see tears in her eyes. She almost never cried. He walked over and gave her a hug. She kissed him on the head, then pulled back the covers and helped him in. He wanted to tell her about what really happened that night on Eagle Lake, but when he started to, she said, "Shhh, it's late. Time for sleep." Max felt himself sink back into silence. She tugged the covers up to his neck. "Sweet dreams."

Later, lying in the dark, Max began to remember even more about the night his father died. Again his body went rigid, just as it had on the landing. Tears dripped down his cheeks. It felt like if he didn't do something, his heart would explode. He sat up, switched on a lamp, and found his sketchbook.

9.

THE ONLY SIGN of Dr. Corwin's growing impatience was the repeated clicking of his ballpoint pen.

"I don't get it," he said. "Last week we had a great talk. Now you're giving me the silent treatment again. How come?"

Max showed no sign that he had even heard him.

Dr. Corwin poked his glasses back on his nose and gazed out the window. Across the courtyard, a janitor was taping a cardboard turkey in a Pilgrim's hat to the cafeteria window. The doctor jammed a pinky into his hairy ear-hole and wiggled it.

Out of nowhere, Max murmured, "Because you won't believe me."

Excited to hear his voice again, Dr. Corwin sat forward. "Why do you say that?"

"Because it's true."

"No, it isn't. I'll believe you. We're friends. Friends believe each other."

"We're not friends. You're just a doctor who wants to find out if I'm crazy. If you believed what I told you last time, you wouldn't be trying to make me tell it to you all over again."

Their eyes met.

They both knew he was right.

Corwin creaked forward even farther in his chair. "Look, it doesn't really matter whether or not I believe you. All that matters is that you tell the truth. Your truth. All the time. No matter what. You'll feel better. More confident. I promise."

Max looked down at his sketch pad and thought it over. In a way, it was pretty much the same advice Lewis had given him.

"My dad didn't jump in the lake," Max whispered. "And it wasn't an accident either. He fell in the water because my stepdad Jim beat him up. He was my dad's business partner then. He kicked my dad into the water."

Dr. Corwin blinked a few times, and then, moving his hands ever so slightly, as though he were afraid a sudden motion might startle Max back to silence, he picked up his notepad, clicked his pen, and scribbled something.

"I'm listening," he said.

Max spoke calmly, merely relaying the facts: "It was late at night. At the old dock on Eagle Lake. They were arguing about money. My dad said Jim was stealing from the business."

"What were *you* doing there?"

"My dad said he was going to the grocery store. I

wanted to go with him. He usually said yes, but this time he didn't. So I snuck into his van. He didn't even know I was there."

"You witnessed everything from inside the van?"

"Yes."

"When did it stop being words? When did it turn violent?"

"When my dad said he was gonna call the police. He walked away, and Jim ran up and punched him really hard. Right here." Max pointed to his own temple. "My dad fell down on his knees. Then Jim kicked him, and he fell into the water. It wasn't very deep. Jim jumped in to help him, but when he pulled him out, there was blood all over his face. He must have hit his head on a rock. Jim got scared and dropped him back in."

"What happened next?" Dr. Corwin asked, writing as fast as he could.

"I ran out to help him, but Jim grabbed me. He said it was too late. He said my dad slipped and drowned. I told him it wasn't true, that I saw what he did. Jim said when the police came, I better tell them my dad slipped and fell, or they'd throw me in jail for lying. He called me crazy and threw me back in the van. I banged my head and started crying. He screamed 'Shut up! Shut up!'"

Max drew a painful breath.

"Then what?" Dr. Corwin asked, looking up but still writing.

"He drove away and left me there. I ran home. I wanted to tell my mom what happened, but I was too scared. I wanted it to be just a dream. I wanted my dad to still be alive. When I woke up in the morning, I heard a man downstairs talking to my mom. I ran down. There were two policemen."

"Did you tell them what happened?"

Max shook his head.

"Did you tell anyone?"

"Never."

"Not even your mother?"

"No."

"How did you feel when everyone said his death was an accident?"

"Mad."

"Some people even said your dad killed himself, didn't they?"

Max nodded slowly, his eyes growing larger and sadder.

"How did you feel when your mom married Jim?"

"Afraid."

"Are you still afraid of him?"

Max nodded again.

"What gave you the courage to tell me the truth?"

"He's doing it again."

"What do you mean?"

"He was screaming at my mom last night. He's trying to steal our college money so he can buy the house."

Dr. Corwin slowly closed his notebook. Max had never seen his face look so old and serious. "I've heard every word you said, Max, and I believe you. It was smart to tell me what happened. And brave. Before I call the police, I'm going to make sure you and your family are protected and safe. I'll contact—"

Max interrupted: "Do it now please. If you wait, he could buy the house."

"I'm sorry, what house?"

"This one."

Max opened his sketch pad and held up his drawing from their first session.

"Oh . . . yes . . . of course." Dr. Corwin flipped back through his notebook until he found the right page. "The Addisons."

"Yeah. No one knows they live there except me. If Jim buys the house and makes it into apartments, they'll have nowhere to go. They might disappear."

"Why doesn't anyone else know they live there?"

"Nobody else can see them."

Dr. Corwin didn't move a muscle. When he spoke, it was one slow word at a time. "Why do you think that is?" He ever so carefully opened to a fresh page in his pad.

Max bit his lip as he considered. "Because— Well . . . Because they might be ghosts."

Dr. Corwin just blinked.

Max saw it. "You promised you'd believe me."

Dr. Corwin's tone was lilting and sweet, like a patient pre-school teacher's. "I believe that *you* believe it." He tilted back in his chair. "Tell me more about the Addisons. Let's start with Grampy."

When Max emerged from Dr. Corwin's office, rather than go straight to Social Studies as he had been instructed to do, he slipped past the hall monitor and escaped out the front door. Classmates, spotting him through the playground fence, yelled stupid jokes at him, about jail breaks and chasing ice cream trucks, but Max pretended not to hear. After telling Dr. Corwin all about the Addisons and seeing the worry and disbelief behind his smile, Max had begun to doubt himself again.

When he burst into the Addison's kitchen, Lizzie stood at the counter, preparing egg salad sandwiches. He walked over and took her hands firmly in his. They felt rough and warm and real. Lizzie smiled at him the way she always did. She didn't seem to notice that he was squeezing her hands.

"Just about to feed my hungry men," she said. "Go on in. They'll be glad to see you."

Max moved to the swinging door, but Lizzie stopped him: "You didn't happen to see Billy playing outside?"

With a hint of sadness, Max shook his head.

In the living room, Grampy and Lewis were playing checkers and talking about the chances of another war in

Europe. Max wished he could tell them that World War Two was definitely going to happen, in less than a year, and that America would join the war and help win it, but he knew if he did that, *they'd* think he was crazy too, and there was only so much pain he could take.

From upstairs, Max heard the sound of Bobby's laughter.

He decided to follow it.

As he had never ventured to the second floor before, Max got momentarily lost, but a sputtering laugh guided him to a door. He peeked inside and saw Bobby lying on an old-fashioned iron bed, reading a comic book.

"Knock-knock," Max said.

Bobby jumped up, scared to death. "Oh, hey, Max. I thought you were Billy. He hates when I touch his stuff. Have you read this one? 'Mickey Mouse, the Sheriff of Nugget Gulch?' It's pretty darned hilarious."

Max dropped his backpack to the floor and settled on the window seat. He scratched Fala's head.

"What's the matter?" Bobby asked.

"What do you mean?"

"Something's eatin' at you. I know that much."

"It's adults, I guess. They never believe kids. Even when we swear we're telling the truth."

"I know what you mean. Once me and Billy were hangin' around outside Peacock's and—"

"What's Peacock's?"

Bobby smirked at Max as though he had to be

kidding. "Duh. The ice cream parlor. Where the streetcar stops on Maple."

"Oh, right."

"And this guy bumps into Mrs. Backer, my old first-grade teacher, and she drops all her packages. And when he's helpin' her pick 'em up, we see this rusty, old revolver stickin' out of his belt. The second he's gone, we run straight to the police station and tell Sergeant Morrow about the gun, only he didn't believe us. He said we had 'overactive imaginations.' Can you believe that?"

"I definitely can."

"Anyway, guess what happened. The next day, the bank over in Lakeville got robbed. And the guy who did it?"

Max's eye flew wide open. "Was the guy with the gun?"

"Probably."

As Max mounted the steps to his house, he was surprised by a car horn.

"Hey, cutie! Time for our field trip! Get in!"

Angela was sitting behind the wheel of her little red car. Paul was sitting next to her, talking on the phone. Max shed his backpack onto the porch and ran to her. As he got in back, Max heard Paul say, "So we can stay with you the whole first week?"

Angela quickly shushed him.

Fastening his seat belt, Max asked, "Are you guys going away somewhere?"

"Yes," Angela replied. "To Harms Woods. With you. Right now. To see the leaves."

As they whizzed north under a bright, blue sky, Paul kept whispering things to Angela, but she cut him off every time, more and more annoyed. Max figured they were going on some sort of secret vacation together.

At Harms Woods, they parked in a big lot and walked across a brown meadow toward the trees. They were just as Angela had described them.

"Look at the colors!" she cried. "It's insane. It's like we're trapped in a cartoon!"

Max laughed. "You were right. They're screaming their heads off. 'Look at me! Look at me!'"

She laughed, and they started to run.

Paul lagged behind, talking again on his phone.

When they finally settled on a bench to rest, Max said, "Are you guys going on a vacation or something?"

"Well," Angela said, "it's sort of a good news/bad news sorta thing. Which do you want first?"

"The good news, I guess."

"We sent our demo—that's, like, a recording of our best music—to my uncle's friend Tony Cermak in Chicago."

Paul, walking up, took over: "He liked it so much, he's hiring us to open for one of his bands. It won't make us rich or anything, but we'll make enough to survive and get tons of exposure."

"And we'll be doing what we love," Angela added. "Which is the most important thing."

"What's the *bad* news?" Max asked, already girding himself.

Angela took his hand. "We have to move to Chicago for a while. We're gonna stay at a friend's the first week, then find a place of our own. We have to leave tomorrow."

"Thank God," Paul said. "Working for my dad has been the worst experience of my life."

"We're gonna miss you *so much*," Angela said.

Max looked down and said nothing.

Sensing his pain, Angela pulled him to his feet.

They all went back to walking, but she had her arm around his shoulder now. To cheer him up, she pointed out the colors of the leaves and made up funny names for them. Envious Green. Door Hinge Orange. Impossible Purple. But he didn't even pretend to care. What did it matter if the world was beautiful if it hurt so much to be alive?

"Oh, come on, it's not like we're *dying,*" Angela said. "We'll visit you all the time."

"I know. I'm just—"

"What? Tell me."

"I don't wanna be alone with Jim."

"Alone?" Paul said, confused. "You'll have Sally and your mom. You'll be fine."

"No, I won't," Max whispered.

It was all he could do not to start crying.

"Something's really the matter," Angela said. "What is it?" Angela sat him down on a big rock. "We're not going anywhere till you tell us."

The words tumbled out.

He told them everything that happened at Eagle Lake.

As the story unfolded, Angela squeezed his hand harder and harder. By the end, she was holding him in both arms. She threw a frightened look at Paul, who didn't say a word.

"You believe me?" Max said.

"Of course," she said, kissing the part in his hair.

Max looked at Paul.

Paul smiled in a strange, heartbroken way. "Sounds like my dad, all right."

"Dr. Corwin, the school psychiatrist, believes me too. He's gonna call the police soon. I'm just worried if Jim finds out—"

Angela hugged him even tighter. "He won't. Nothing's going to happen to you, I promise."

"You won't go to Chicago?"

"Not yet," Angela said. "Not till we know you're safe. Not till he's in jail."

10.

ON THE WAY BACK from Harms Woods, Angela pulled into a roadside restaurant, ablaze with neon. It was so late they decided to eat in the car. Sitting in the back seat, too nervous to take even take a bite of his burger, Max watched Angela and Paul eat theirs in near silence. When either of them spoke, it was something short and random. Max knew they were frightened.

Later, as they sped home, leaning his head on the window and watching cars whiz by so close that one jerk of the wheel would mean certain death, Max half-wished it would happen. If only Dr. Corwin had already called the police, then Jim would be in jail right now. But he hadn't, and Jim wasn't. In the real world hardly anything ever happened the way it should.

When they pulled into the driveway, Angela reached across and touched Paul's face. They looked at each other and neither spoke for a few long seconds, until finally Angela whispered, "I'm sorry." Max knew what she meant. She was sorry Paul's father was such a terrible person.

When they got out of the car, Max ran over and took Angela's hand. It made no sense that he looked to her instead of to Paul for protection—what could she do against a man Jim's size?—but for some reason no one made him feel safer than she did.

As they walked toward the house, Max saw something move in an upstairs window. He stopped and watched as Jim's huge silhouette filled the white curtain.

"What's the matter?" Angela asked.

Too afraid to speak, Max eventually pointed.

Angela looked up, but Jim's shadow was already gone.

"What?" she said. "I don't see anything."

"He's waiting for me. He knows I snitched."

"No way. How could he know?"

"What if Dr. Corwin told the police, and the police told Jim?"

"They'd never do that."

Max relaxed slightly, but he was still unsure.

Paul, ahead of them now, pushed open the front door.

By the time Max and Angela stepped inside the house, Paul was already running up the stairs.

"Wait!" Angela cried out. "What are you doing?"

"Stay," he commanded.

Max and Angela looked at each other. Before either of them could speak, Caroline entered from the dining room, drying her hands with a dish towel. As usual, she was smiling with kindness and hope, but Max could tell something was terribly wrong. Her eyes were red as though she'd been crying.

"I baked an apple-rhubarb pie," she said.

Paul found his father in his little study, sitting on the edge of the desk, lighting a cigarette, wearing a smug smile.

"What's up, kid? Something on your mind?"

"I know what you did," Paul said, closing the door behind him.

"Is that right?"

"Tom didn't fall in the lake. You knocked him out. You kicked him into the water. Instead of calling for help, you let him drown."

"You believe that?"

"Yeah, I do. He threatened to turn you in, didn't he? He caught you stealing from the business. That's why you left him to die."

Jim took a drag of his cigarette, deeper than usual, and let the smoke ooze out through his nostrils and smile.

Paul's face twisted with contempt. "We'll see how funny the cops think it is."

"Might as well give 'em the *whole* story then."

Paul froze with his hand on the doorknob. "What's that mean?"

Smoke still leaking from his face, Jim fell into the desk chair and grabbed a pad of yellow paper, filled with scrawl. "I had a talk with the school shrink today. This Corwin guy. I wrote down everything he said." He pointed with his cigarette at a chair. "Sit."

Rigid with suspicion, Paul obeyed.

Jim spoke lightheartedly, as though sharing good news. "Seems the little dummy went in there today and told Corwin the same crazy story he told you. And he actually believed him. He was ready to turn me in. But then Max told him another story. About a family of ghosts living in that old house I want to buy."

"*What?*"

"Exactly what I said. Max even dragged Monroe over there so he could see the ghosts for himself. Only it didn't work out as planned. Turns out Max is the only one who can see 'em. I said, 'Doc, are you telling me my stepson's a loony tune?' He said professionals don't talk that way. He said Max suffers from—" Jim consulted his notes: "'—a delusional psychotic disorder.' But he said there's hope. They've got these wonder drugs now. But it's best to take 'em under controlled conditions. He wants to put Max in the hospital for a week or two." He consulted his notes again. "St. Francis Children's Hospital over in Vernon. Psych ward."

"You wouldn't do that."

"Why wouldn't I? Doctor's orders."

"You'll need Caroline's permission."

"Already got it." He held up a typed document. "She fought it at first. You know mothers and their babies. But I got her to see it's no time to be selfish."

Paul found the rest of his family sitting in tense silence around the kitchen table. Sally was holding her mother's hand, something Paul had never seen.

"I had Max tell them everything," Angela said. "I think we should all go to a motel now. In the morning, we'll go to the police."

Showing no sign that he had even heard her, Paul knelt in front of Max. "Did you tell Dr. Corwin that there are ghosts living in Mr. Monroe's house?"

Suddenly, there wasn't a sound in the room but the hum of the refrigerator.

One by one, Max looked at their confused faces. He wanted so badly tell them no, that it was just a silly story he had made up to prank the doctor. But telling the truth was what had finally got him to start talking again. If he lied, he might fall silent forever.

Max met Paul's eyes and slowly nodded.

Paul dropped his head, defeated.

"Actual ghosts or make-believe ones?" Angela said.

"Both, I guess. I mean, they're not real like *we* are. They're much happier. All they do all day is eat cookies, play music, and drink tea. And they never fight. But they're not just make-believe either. They're Mr.

Monroe's family who died in a fire when he was about my age. They've been waiting for him to come home ever since."

No one spoke.

Max could sense they didn't believe him. He didn't blame them.

Finally his mother spoke: "What you saw Jim do to Dad at Eagle Lake. Was that real? As real as the ghosts are?"

Max knew what she was thinking, but it was too late to turn back. He nodded solemnly. Like a balloon losing air, Angela slumped in her chair. Sally covered her face with her hands. Caroline started to cry. Max knew it was over. They would never trust him again. Only one other person in the world knew he was telling the truth about Eagle Lake, and his heavy boots were shaking the floor upstairs.

Just before dawn, in the greenish glow of his nightlight, Max lay sound asleep on his stomach. He did not hear the creak of the door or the footsteps crossing to his bed. He woke up only when a hand touched his neck. He gasped and flipped over, terrified.

"Just came to say good-bye," Paul whispered.

"Why? Where're you going?"

"Chicago."

"But you said you wouldn't until—"

"I know, but after what I said to my dad last night . . . what I accused him of . . . I've got no choice really. Pretty hard to take back. Anyway, it's for the best. It's time for me to grow the hell up."

"Take me with you," Max said.

"Dude, I wish I could. But that's kidnapping."

"You can't leave me alone with him."

"You're not alone. You have your mom and Sally. You'll be okay."

"*They* can't stop him! Where . . . where's Angie?"

"In the car. She wanted to say good-bye to you, but she's a huge crier. She didn't want to make a scene. She'll call you in a little bit."

Resigned, Max settled back on his pillow.

Paul ruffled his hair. "Anyway, time to hit the road."

He rose and headed for the door.

"Wait!" Max sat up and grabbed his sketchbook. He ripped out a bunch of pages, folded them up, and handed them to Paul.

"Give these to her, okay?"

"Sure thing." Paul slipped them in his coat pocket. "See you soon. At Christmas."

Max smiled bravely, but there were still tears in his eyes. "Better skedaddle now."

Paul made a face, surprised by the word.

"Lewis says 'skedaddle,'" Max explained. "He's Mr. Monroe's father. He lives in the house."

After Paul and Angela had driven away, Max somehow fell back asleep. He dreamt that he was walking down a street on a spring day. The bright green lawns were bursting with weird black-and-white flowers. He decided to stop and pick one for his mother. As he bent down, with no warning at all, not even a rumble, the earth opened up like a giant mouth, and he fell inside. Suddenly he was the tiniest thing in the universe, falling through a reddish void bigger than anything he had ever see or even imagined. Then bang! He was awake, staring at the blank ceiling. He looked around. Morning sun burned in the windows. The clock said 10:03. He heard voices downstairs. His mother's, Jim's, and a third one he didn't recognize at first. When he realized whose it was, he bolted for the door, but then, remembering, he ran back to his bed.

At the same moment, Jim was setting a stack of documents on the coffee table in front of Mr. Monroe.

"The kids can't wait to move in," Jim said. "They're already fighting over who gets which room."

"Well, there are plenty to go around," Monroe replied.

Jim handed him a fancy gold fountain pen that had belonged to Max's father. Monroe leaned his cane against the chair and slipped on his eyeglasses.

Jim and Caroline smiled at each other.

As Monroe lowered the gold tip of the pen to the first signature line, he heard, "Billy?"

He turned his head, and there was Max standing at the door in his pajamas, clutching something against his chest.

"Why, good morning, Max," Monroe said.

"I have a present for you."

"You do? How kind."

"He's always been so generous," Caroline said. "When he was three years old, he emptied out his whole piggy bank just to buy Tom a Father's Day present. I mean, how many kids that age even understand the meaning—"

Jim lifted a hand, silencing her.

He said: "We're busy now, son. Pour yourself some cereal, and we'll come get you later."

Monroe smiled at Jim. "I'd like to accept my gift first, if you don't mind."

"What? Oh, yeah, okay. I just thought—"

Seizing the opportunity, Max walked over and handed Monroe the object he was clutching to his chest.

"And what's this?" Monroe said, his eyes shining with anticipation as he opened Max's sketchbook.

The first drawing was of the house on Arcadia Lane.

"You drew this yourself?"

Max nodded.

"Will you look at that? You have quite an eye, young man."

"Thank you."

Monroe turned to the next sketch. When he saw it, he was too shocked to speak.

"Bobby's room," Max said.

"Bobby?" Caroline asked. "Who's that?"

"His twin brother. Bobby was born three minutes after Mr. Monroe, but you couldn't tell."

Monroe, as though in a trance, turned to the next sketch.

"And who are these funny people?" Caroline said, moving closer.

"Mr. Monroe's parents. And his grandfather. They died in the fire. They live in the house now, waiting for him to come home. If the house is carved up, they'll have nowhere to go."

Jim sputtered a nervous laugh. "Carved up? What're you talkin' about? Nobody's carvin' up anything." He moved Max aside and muttered to Monroe: "We're checking him into the hospital Monday morning. Psych ward. His mind's not right."

"I'm not crazy!" Max insisted. "They just *think* I am because I can see your family!"

Jim snapped his fingers at Caroline. "Enough with the ghost stories! Get him outta here!"

Max lunged past Jim and grabbed Monroe by the arm. "I'm telling the truth! How do I know everything about them if I can't see them?"

The old man looked as though he might burst out

crying. His lip and hand trembled. His voice was hoarse. "Perhaps you saw photographs . . . or found an old newspaper at the library. Or your imagination, it's overactive . . . it's—"

Caroline took Max firmly by the shoulder. "Come on, baby. Let's get you some breakfast."

As she led him away, Max's eyes flew open with a new idea. He whipped his head around. "That's what they said when you and Bobby saw the guy with the rusty revolver in front of Peacock's. You told Sergeant Morrow about the gun, but he didn't believe you. He said you had an overactive imagination! Then there was a bank robbery in Lakeview, and it was probably the same guy!"

Monroe could not have looked more astonished.

"That's it!" Jim grabbed Max by the arm and shoved him toward the stairs. *"Go to your room!"*

"I can't sign these," Monroe said, setting down the pen.

Jim wheeled around in disbelief.

With the help of his cane, Monroe struggled to his feet. "I need to pay my home one last visit. I'll take Max with me, if that's all right with you."

Jim's face reddened.

The vein appeared between his eyes.

It was useless to argue.

11.

AS THEY WALKED TOGETHER, William Monroe spoke quietly of small things: the blueness of the morning sky, the cold start to November, the countless ways, good and bad, the neighborhood had changed since his childhood. Max was so nervous that he heard barely a word of what he said. He knew this visit was his last chance to be believed. If it went as badly as the first, the house would be sold, and he'd be locked away in a hospital, maybe forever.

When they arrived in front, Max took Monroe by the hand.

"The back door's always open. They walked carefully down the side path, with Monroe leading the way, pushing aside branches with his cane while Max stomped down weeds.

"I think maybe you couldn't see them last time because you were afraid to," Max suggested hopefully.

When Monroe merely smiled, Max knew he still didn't believe him.

In the backyard, Max held his breath and then ever so slowly laid his foot on the porch.

The lights popped on and the music played.

Just as slowly, Max looked at Monroe.

Nothing. His face hadn't changed.

"You don't hear the music?"

Monroe shook his head.

Max felt like crying. Seeing what no one else could see was like a curse. The worst thing that had ever happened to him. For the first time, he actually wished he had never stepped foot in the place. Head down, Max walked to the door and opened it. The smell of baking cookies wafted out.

"Do you wanna come in again? Or just forget it?"

Monroe opened his mouth to speak, but stopped before making a sound. His hand twitched, as though it had been given a tiny electric shock.

Max looked at him, alarmed. "Are you okay?"

The old man's milky blue eyes pooled with tears. "Raisin molasses pinwheels."

"You smell them?" Max asked.

Monroe nodded. And then suddenly his mouth and eyes opened as wide as they possibly could.

"The music?"

Again Monroe nodded, his face a mask of wonder.

Heart bursting, Max grabbed Monroe's hand and pulledhim across the porch to the door.

Lizzie wasn't in the kitchen, but the sheet of pinwheel cookies lay on the wooden table.

"Take one!" Max said. "They won't mind!"

With a trembling hand, Monroe picked up one of the cookies. When he bit into it, he closed his eyes. From the sounds he made, it was as though each chew brought back a memory.

Impatient, Max pulled Monroe through the swinging doors. This time, Max did not need to narrate. Walking slowly through the house, the old man gazed with love at the gleaming oak floors, the crystal lamp, the old-fashioned telephone, the starched, white tablecloth, and the silver candlesticks. He strummed his fingertips across the face of the grandfather clock.

"A miracle," was the only thing he said, over and over again.

In the living room, Max unfolded the newspaper. "See how new it looks? But look at the date. November 11, 1938."

"The date of the fire," Monroe said.

"I knew it!" Max cried happily.

The music from the parlor grew louder.

Max ran across the long room and shouted "Surprise!" as he yanked opened the French doors, bursting with pride.

The family immediately stopped playing.

Fala jumped off the window seat and scampered over to greet Max.

"There's the boy," Grampy said.

"Welcome!" said Lewis.

"Where ya been?" Bobby asked.

Max wasn't sure if they were talking to him or to Monroe, who was now standing at his side. He got his answer straight away, when Lizzie abruptly stood, smoothing down the front of her dress.

"You've brought a friend with you, she said. "Well, I wished you'd warned me."

Grampy stepped forward. "Welcome. I'm George Addison. This is my son Lewis."

Lewis tipped an invisible cap.

"Tickling the ivories is his wife Lizzie."

"Pleasure," Lizzie said.

"And last but not least, manning the licorice stick is my grandson Bobby. His brother Billy plays the trombone, but he's out and about somewhere."

"Don't you know who this is?" Max asked.

"Can't say that I do," Grampy replied, holding out his hand to Monroe.

Overcome with emotion, Monroe took it.

"You all right, friend?" Grampy asked, looking into his eyes. "I don't believe I caught your name."

Monroe tried to speak but couldn't do it without crying.

"It's Billy!" Max proclaimed. "Bobby's twin brother!"

"Looks more like *my* twin," Grampy said.

When the family laughed, Max's face reddened. "It's the truth!" He spun around to Monroe. "Tell 'em, Billy!"

Monroe, his hands trembling terribly, pulled Max aside. He bent down as far as he was able. "Don't be mad. They're waiting for a nine-year-old boy. Of course they don't recognize me. How could they?"

Monroe straightened up and addressed the family in his steadiest voice. "Friends, my name is, in fact, William Addison. Max assumed that I was the person you were waiting for. An honest mistake, I think."

Max was upset by Monroe's lie, but before he could object, Lizzie rose from the bench.

"Please stay for tea. Billy will be home any minute now. I'm sure he'd love to meet his namesake."

When Monroe hesitated, Max asked urgently, "You'll stay, right? *Please?*"

Monroe addressed the family again, doing his best not to cry. "Thank you so much for the invitation, but I'm afraid I have another engagement. It's been such a pleasure to meet you all. How kind you all are. What beautiful music you make. Max will show me to the door. Then he'll return and enjoy a cup of tea."

Caught by another surge of emotion, which he valiantly resisted, Monroe went around the room, hugging each of them. They smiled at him strangely, wondering why this complete stranger seemed to be filled with so much warm feeling for them. When Monroe reached Bobby, his self-control finally broke. He let out a strange, strangled cry and pressed Bobby to his legs, holding on as though he would never let go. Everyone, including Max, was paralyzed, unsure what to do.

"I can hardly breathe," Bobby squeaked at last.

Everyone laughed, including Monroe, and he let Bobby go.

In the kitchen, Max beseeched his friend. "Why do you want to leave? We just got here. Don't you want to convince them who you are?"

Monroe, his tears drying, struggled to explain. "The last time they saw me I kissed them goodnight . . . Mama reminded me to brush my teeth and say my prayers . . . and I ran upstairs to bed. All these years they've waited for that same little boy to come running *down* the stairs. Obviously, that's impossible. We'll be reunited soon enough. I know that now." He laid a big, flat hand on Max's shoulder. "You're a special boy, gifted with mighty powers. Never doubt your eyes. Or your imagination. Do you promise me that?"

Max nodded, smiling.

Monroe moved slowly to the door.

"Where are you going now?" Max asked.

"I have some important business to attend to."

Speeding toward Chicago, Angela smiled at her bandmates. Driving their van in the next lane over, Ronny Foster thrashed his long hair to the music blaring from the stereo, while his brother Rick stood on the passenger seat with half his body out of the sunroof, singing along and pumping a defiant fist.

Angela shouted: "Wait till we're famous before you start acting like idiots!"

They both shook their heads no.

She laughed and rolled up the window.

"Excellent advice," Paul said.

"Thanks."

"You're not just hot. You're wise."

"I'd kiss you for that compliment, but I can smell your beef-jerky breath from here."

"I've got mints in my jacket."

Angela reached into the back seat. As she lifted his jacket, folded papers fell out.

"Oh, that's a present from Max," Paul said.

She picked them up. "Why didn't you tell me?"

"I just did."

Annoyed, she unfolded the pages. The first drawing made her smile. It showed a rippling lake on a moonlit night. The next one dissolved her smile. As she flipped the pages, she was gripped by fear.

"Good stuff?" Paul asked casually. When she didn't answer, he looked over. "What's wrong?"

"Pull over."

"Why?"

"Just do it."

Paul honked twice to alert the brothers, then skidded to a gravelly stop on the shoulder.

Angela showed him the drawings.

The second was of two men arguing on a dock.

"That's your dad, right? And Tom?"

Paul nodded.

In the next, Jim punched Tom from behind.

In the next, he kicked him.

In the last, Tom splashed into the water.

"What's the big deal?" Paul said. "It's exactly what he said happened."

"But look at the detail. He even drew your dad's belt buckle. His boots. It's so *alive*."

"He has an incredible imagination. You know that."

"What if it's not imagination? What if it's memory? What if he made up the story about the ghosts to help him deal with this horrible thing he really *did* see? Maybe Jim only wants him in the hospital to keep him quiet about it. Shouldn't we at least tell the police his story? Let them investigate? Isn't that the least we can do?"

Jim did his best not to appear overeager, but his eyes were panicked and his brow shone with sweat as he led Monroe back to the sale documents.

"Where's Max?" Caroline asked, entering from the kitchen.

"Honey, quiet. Plenty of time for chit-chat later. Sit right down, my friend."

"He's still at the house," Monroe answered, staring at the documents, but declining to sit.

"He's there all alone?" she asked.

"Hardly. He's enjoying a cup of tea with my family."

Monroe took a moment to enjoy the confusion on both their faces.

"Like you," he continued, "I assumed that Max's imagination had gotten the best of him, but I know better now. Which is why I won't sell you my house, Jim. It wouldn't be fair to the occupants."

"*Occupants?* It's empty!"

"Oh, no. It's home to a family of ghosts. Or, if you prefer, living memories. Of kindness, generosity, and love."

"What the hell are you talking about? That's just . . . it's just crazy! I'm offering you just what you asked for."

"I suspect it's *your* head that ought to be examined. Pretending to love an old man's home just so you can destroy it for profit? I pity you, sir. As I do this poor woman, who stands by you out of nothing but fear. I pray you both see the error of your ways. Good day."

Monroe turned and, hardly using his cane, walked out the door.

Jim didn't move a muscle. Then he turned around and glared at Caroline. Reading his terrible anger, she shrank away, backing into a corner.

"It isn't my fault," she pleaded.

"I know exactly whose fault it is."

Jim marched into the pantry to get out the bottle of Scotch he had bought for their celebration.

12.

ANYONE GIFTED WITH Max's power of sight who stood across the street that night would have seen a rectangle of golden light magically open up in the center of the boarded-up front door, as Max, zipping up his jacket, emerged. Behind him, filling the doorway, Grampy and Lewis, appeared, waving good-bye. As Max descended the stairs, the rectangle of light shrank and disappeared, returning the house to darkness.

Hours earlier, when Monroe had told Max he had business to attend to, Max had known what he meant: he was backing out of the deal with Jim. As happy as this made him, Max knew there would be dire consequences. The thought of returning home to Jim was so scary that Max had extended his visit for as long as he could. When it was almost ten o'clock and the Addisons began to yawn, he had no choice but to leave.

Max arrived home to find the first floor dark, but for a dim glow beneath the kitchen door. He pushed it open and was surprised to see no one there. On the table sat his dinner, covered in plastic, next to a glass of grape juice. He sat down and ate in perfect silence. He heard no distant voices or even a footstep from upstairs. Had Jim taken his mother and Sally out to dinner? That only made sense if Mr. Monroe had gone ahead with the sale, and they were celebrating, but that was impossible, wasn't it?

Uncertain, Max climbed the stairs to the second floor as quietly as he could. His plan was to slip into bed unnoticed and hope that in the morning everything would somehow be better. At the landing, he heard laughter from Sally's TV. He walked to her door and turned the knob, but it was locked. He walked on and stopped when he saw that his mother and Jim's door was open a few inches.

He tiptoed over and peeked inside.

His mother, wearing her prettiest nightgown, sat at the edge of the bed with her head down. Her hair was damp and stringy. She was as still as a statue. In the reflection of the mirror behind her, Max spotted Jim standing with his back turned, holding a half-empty liquor bottle. His arm rose up. He put the bottle to his lips. His Adam's apple jerked as he guzzled. He lowered the bottle and wiped his mouth with his hairy forearm.

"Whimpering and whining," he mumbled. "Why? What the hell did you lose? I lost *everything.*"

His mother's voice was hoarse. "He didn't know what he was doing. Please don't punish him. He's such a good boy."

"If *I* did something like that, my old man would have tanned my ass good." Jim yanked the curtains aside and looked down at the street. "Where is the little freak, anyway?"

"Don't call him that."

"I'll call him whatever I please!"

Terrified, Max stepped away from the door. Jim's eyes looked the same as they had the night on Eagle Lake. So angry they were barely human. He tiptoed quickly away. He stopped at Sally's door and tapped with one finger.

"Leave me alone!" she screamed.

She thought he was Jim.

Certain that Jim had heard the scream, Max ducked into the hall closet. He sank to the floor beneath a shelf of folded sheets and towels. In the darkness, smelling of mothballs, he waited, eyes pressed shut, heart racing, waiting to hear Jim's heavy boots thunder down the hall.

A long minute passed.

Then another.

There was only his own heartbeat and the distant laughter of Sally's television.

Max cracked the door and looked. Nothing had changed, except that his mother and Jim's door was shut now. Maybe Jim was so drunk that he hadn't heard Sally shout. Max held his breath and walked as quickly as he could to his own bedroom. He slipped inside. It was only after he had closed the door that he heard it. A low growl. Max whipped around. Jim sat on the bed, his huge body making it seem miniature. His eyes were dull and blurry. He patted the comforter.

"Come here, kid. Let's talk."

His voice was so soft that it was even scarier than if it had been loud.

"My chance to be somebody," Jim muttered, shaking his head. "Make you all proud. *Me* proud. We'd have been rich. But you . . . you just had to—"

Realizing that Jim was drunker than he had ever seen him, Max began to back out of the room. When Jim noticed this, his mouth twisted and he lunged off the bed, reaching out clenched hands as though to grab Max by the face. Max spun around and darted away. He ran down the hall and threw himself on Sally's door.

"Let me in! Let me in!" he screamed.

He heard Jim stagger into the hallway.

"Sally! Hurry!" Max shrieked.

He heard her fumbling with the lock as Jim charged down the hall. The door opened too late, so Max dropped to the floor and dove between Jim's legs. Jim grabbed him by the shirt.

"Leave him alone!" Sally shouted.

She shoved Jim, knocking him down.

Max's shirt ripped.

Max managed to scramble away. He regained his feet and ran for his mother's room. Sally ran after him as Jim climbed unsteadily to his feet. Sally skidded past their mom's door. Max grabbed her by the T-shirt and jerked them both inside. They slammed and locked the door. A moment later, Jim punched it so hard that Max was knocked to his knees.

"Don't make me break it down!" Jim bellowed. "I'm counting to five! One! Two!"

"What do we do?" Max whispered to Sally.

"I don't know!" Sally said.

"Three! Four!"

They braced themselves against the door, eyes squeezed shut.

Like a miracle, Jim grumbled, "I need a drink," and his boots clomped away.

Max and Sally turned around and saw their mother sitting on the floor near the window. She clutched her phone.

"Did you call the police?" Max asked.

She wildly shook her head, but then, as though the mere question had given her the courage she needed, she punched out 9-1-1. When the operator picked up, she spoke slowly, trying not to cry. "My husband's been drinking . . . he's violent . . . I'm scared . . . my children are in the house."

Suddenly, Jim's boots returned.

"I warned you!" he shouted.

As before, Max and Sally closed their eyes and pressed themselves against the door.

A moment later, it exploded. The kids were flung to the floor. Pieces of wood and metal from the lock flew past them.

Jim stepped in, smiling like he had just won

something, as though mere brutality were something to be proud of.

"127 Overlook Road!" Caroline screamed into the phone.

Alarmed, Jim hurried over, wrenched the phone from her hand, and flung it against the wall, where it burst into pieces.

"They're coming!" Sally screamed, standing up, her eyes filled with fury. "How long do you want to go to jail for? You lay a hand on us, you'll *never* get out!"

"No crime to smack your kids."

"We're not your kids!" Max shouted bravely.

Jim moved closer.

Max backed into a corner, trapped.

Sally jumped on Jim's back. Furious, he tried to shake her loose, but she grabbed his hair with one hand and wrapped the other arm around his thick neck. Growling like a bear, he swung her feet into the vanity. Perfume bottles shattered. The mirror crashed to the floor. And still she didn't let go. He swung again, and this time her feet hit the wooden bed frame. She cried out in pain and lost her grip. As she slammed to the floor, Max darted away. Jim lunged for him but was too slow.

Racing down the hallway, Max heard Jim chasing him. He was too afraid to look back. At the stairs, Max tripped, and Jim's huge hands clamped down on his shoulders and swept him off his feet. He screamed, kicking the air as Jim carried him to the railing. He was certain he was about to be thrown over it. But then, directly below them, the front door burst open. Max saw Paul and Angela looking up at him from the foyer.

"Stop it!" Paul shouted, pointing a finger. "Put him down!"

Jim hesitated. Seeing his chance, Max bit down on Jim's thumb as hard as he could. He tasted his salty blood. Jim howled in pain and, staggering backwards, let go of him. As Max hit the floor, he saw Paul charging up the stairs.

A siren wailed in the distance.

Paul stopped ten feet from Jim, arms raised, speaking as calmly as he could. "That's the cops, Dad. They'll sober you up. They'll let you go in the morning. But you gotta end this right now."

Jim glared down at Max on the floor. "You tell 'em I didn't hurt your dad. He fell! Tell 'em what happened!"

Max knew all he had to do was lie, and they would all be safe. He took a deep breath, clenched teeth, and said, *"You killed him."*

Jim was shocked for an instant, then he sneered and drew back a boot to kick Max.

Angela screamed.

Paul lunged at Jim.

Jim pushed Paul away, slamming him into the wall.

"You're a liar!" Jim screamed at Max.

"I'm not!" Max screamed back. *"You killed him! It's the truth!"*

As Jim drew back the boot again, someone appeared out of nowhere and pushed Jim hard. He cried out, staggered back, lost his balance, and toppled over the railing. Arms flailing, he fell through the air and landed with a gigantic, meaty thud.

Max, speechless, spun his head around to see who had saved his life. It was his mother. There was a sharpness in her eye he had not seen since his father died. She gathered him into a fierce hug.

"I love you," she said as she began to cry. "I love you. I love you." Then she said "I'm sorry" the same way, repeating it over and over again.

When Max could finally speak, all he said was "I know, Mama."

13.

ON A GRAY MORNING, smelling of wood fire and approaching snow, two dozen mourners, dressed all in black, gathered at Greenlawn Cemetery to bid farewell to a man who had walked the earth for almost ninety years. William Monroe was not laid to rest alone. Rather, he was buried beneath a white marble headstone, showing the wear of decades, that read simply, "Here Lies a Family."

Max stood with his own family at the open grave, holding Angela's hand. All around them stood Mr. Monroe's friends from the Oakview Retirement Home. Not in attendance was Jim Jarvis, who had been buried a few weeks before with far fewer mourners and without words of comfort like the ones a young minister offered now: "We commit his body to the ground, earth to earth, ashes to ashes, dust to dust, in sure and certain hope of resurrection into the eternal life, through our lord Jesus Christ, who shall cleanse our vile body that it may be like unto his glorious body . . . ."

Max wasn't sure what many of the words meant, but he knew they had something to do with good people living forever.

Later that same afternoon, Max and his family drove to the Addisons' house. As they got out of the car, a harsh voice tore the air: "Hey, Beatty!"

Max spotted Tim Schmidt and Eddie Wong across the street. They were smiling at him as though they were his best friends. Max looked away and quickly back again to see if they disappeared. They did not.

"Yeah?" Max said cautiously.

"Come here for a sec," Tim said.

Max walked over to them.

"I just wanna say I'm, like, you know, sorry for what I said about your dad jumping in the lake."

Ever since the true story of his father's death had appeared in the paper, everyone at school was talking about it—not to Max's face, of course, but he had heard the whispers in the hallways.

"Tim didn't mean it," Eddie explained. "He just likes to talk crap."

"Yeah," Tim agreed, "I talk a lotta crap."

"That's okay," Max said. "Nobody really knew what happened except me."

Caroline shouted: "Honey, hurry up!"

Max shrugged at the boys. "I better go."

"What're you doin' in that old house anyway?" Tim asked. "It's haunted, you know."

"No, it's not. I own it."

They laughed at his joke.

"I'm serious," Max said. "The man who owned it died and gave it to me in his will. Plus enough money to fix it up."

"A kid can own a house?" Tim asked incredulously.

"Yeah, I didn't believe it either."

"Hey, maybe once you're all moved in, we can come over. Play video games or something."

"Maybe."

Max walked away.

"See ya!" Eddie shouted.

By the time Max reached the front porch, his family was already inside. He laid his foot on the first step. Lights popped on in the windows, but no music played.

Entering for the first time in weeks, Max was so happy to be back that he almost forgot he was the only one who could see its beauty.

"Boy," Caroline said, eyeing the devastation. "What a mess."

"I believe this is what's known in real estate circles as a tear-down," Sally said. "Only no way we're gonna."

"It must have really been gorgeous," Angela said. "Look at the woodwork over the door."

Paul stood at the fireplace. "And these tiles. It's just smoke damage. I bet they'll clean up great."

Max heard a noise. He stepped out of the living room and saw Grampy, Lewis, and Lizzie descending the staircase, carrying old-fashioned suitcases. They wore fancy hats.

"Max!" Grampy said.

"We were afraid we'd miss you," Lewis said.

"Where are you going?" Max asked.

"A little trip," Lizzie said.

"To where?"

No one answered.

Grampy slapped a hand on Max's shoulder. "Good news. You'll never guess."

"What?" Max asked.

The answer came in thumps on the landing, where Bobby appeared with his identical twin. They were impossible to tell apart, and they each carried the same khaki duffel.

"Hey, Maxie!" cried Bobby.

The brothers bounded down the stairs together, with Fala trotting at their heels.

Bobby gave Max a little punch on the arm and said to Billy, "This is the kid I was telling you about."

"Nice to meet you, Max," Billy said.

Max looked deeply and thought he saw in the boy's gentle blue eyes the spirit of the old man who had changed his life forever.

"Nice to meet you, too."

"We'd better skedaddle," Lewis said.

"We'll miss you, Max," said Lizzie.

Grampy gave him a wink. "You check on the place while we're gone, okay? Keep the raccoons out of the attic."

"I promise," Max said.

"One last thing," Lewis said. "If you don't mind."

Right then, Caroline happened to glance over her shoulder. Her eyes filled with alarm. She gasped and pointed. Paul and Angela looked. By the front door, Max was high on his tiptoes, hugging the air.

The family exchanged worried looks. Had Dr. Corwin been right? Was Max going to have to be put in the hospital, after all?

Something happened next that answered the question forever: Lifted even higher by the hug, Max rose until his sneakers were six inches off the floor.

Never again, in the years that followed, did the family doubt Max's sanity, although sometimes, when they remembered this moment, they doubted their own.

After seeing the Addisons out, Max stood at the open door, watching them go. Grampy led the way with Lewis and Lizzie right behind him. Taking up the rear, the brothers chatted and laughed, playfully banging each other with their bags. Every now and then, Fala barked for no good reason.

Max noticed the most remarkable thing. As they walked, everything ahead of them was just as it had been the morning of the fire. The homes, the cars, the streetlights, the fences, the toys left unattended in the front yards, were all of an earlier time. Even the sky seemed bluer. But behind them, everything they had just passed immediately returned to the present day, back to normal, which in Max's eyes, after all he had been through, was in its own way even more wonderful.

THE END

ALLISON BURNETT is the author of the B.K. Troop trilogy of novels, the first of which, *Christopher*, was a finalist for the 2004 PEN Center USA Literary Award in Fiction. He also wrote and directed film versions of his novels *Undiscovered Gyrl* and *Another Girl*.

Made in the USA
Monee, IL
30 March 2022